NO STRINGS ATTACHED

BY

W PARKS BRIGHAM

NO STRINGS ATTACHED

(Allanville Matchmakers Book #3)

Copyright © 2014 W Parks Brigham

All rights reserved.

ISBN 10: 0984806822

ISBN-13: 9780984806829

Dedication

I would like to dedicate this book to my family
and friends for their love support and
constant encouragement.
Thanks guys!

Acknowledgement

Special thanks to those who have supported me during my
writing career. You are so much appreciated and
loved for all that you have done.

PROLOGUE

"Chancey, are you sure you want to solicit Minerva and her matchmaking team to get involved in this?"

"More than ever, Dexter; mainly because he retired from the Air Force. I'm afraid if this boy doesn't settle down; he's going to end up making a mistake he can't get out of."

"Again, I ask if you want interference from my Minnie. Once you put her on his tail, there's no turning back with her and her ladies. They thrive on this matchmaking stuff."

"How well I know."

Both men chuckled because it was a known fact his Minerva had tried to fix him up with a few seasoned ladies. He'd found her choices to be quite refreshing with him being a widower for some time. But it wasn't about him at the moment. It was about his grandson, who went around calling himself Chocolate Swirl, which sounded like a stripper's name.

"Okay, Chancey, I'll notify her right away."

"Mighty fine, Dexter; see you at the brotherhood's meeting."

CHAPTER ONE

February

"Oh, Ryane, you look absolutely beautiful."

The simple long veil and gown, with flattering lines complemented her plus size figure. Alterations would not be necessary as long as she continued her maintenance weight plan. Like most brides, Ryane had been on a diet and had lost sixty pounds. She could fit into the dream dress she'd secretly had her heart set on.

"Thank you, Mother." She turned around and looked over at her sister Rena, who had turned her nose up at everything Ryane had tried on. She dared her to look down at the one she saved for last, her favorite, especially with the wedding being six weeks away. Ryane wanted a spring wedding, and it was set for March twentieth, the first day of spring. They didn't have time for Rena to be so picky. And most importantly, she loved this dress and was totally pleased with how she looked in it. The fitted bodice flowed into a soft fluid train-less chiffon skirt, with an empire waist accented with exquisite, hand-beaded lace and ruching details. The back was just as gorgeous as the front, with the same jeweled designs. "Rena, what do you think of this one?"
"Ryane, I think this is the one; you look lovely."

They all smiled. Her mother and sister gave her a big hug and then a high five.

"Now that we have that out the way ladies, I must leave good company. I have an errand I must take care of," Rena said.

"Auh, *Little Big Sister*, I thought we could have lunch afterwards," said Ryane, with her face displaying disappointment as well as the sound of her voice.

"I'm sorry, Sis, I have to go. I need to take care of a little business before the storm arrives. Kisses," said Rena, waving goodbye while walking away mumbling she hated that nickname and was glad that was over. She had been bored clean out of her mind and didn't want to see another dress in a size twenty. Really, how many did they have? They'd spent the entire morning and for what, thought Rena. All the dresses her sister tried on looked the same. She was sick of all the hype for Ryane and her big day, she thought with a smirk. All she'd heard was Ryane this, and Ryane that… ughhh. Anyway, what kind of name is that for a woman even if their parents did add the **e** at the end? Rena was glad she was not the first born and stuck with that name. Yes, she loved her daddy dearly but certainly didn't want to be his namesake. It was evident her parents wanted their first child to be a boy. What a disappointment that must have been.

At any rate, back to the issue at hand, thought Rena. If she got her way, her father's namesake would never get to wear that plain dress. Now smiling, all she needed was one more time with him, and she was sure it would happen. It was her time of the month for conception. With a pleased look, Rena thought about her own dress. Unbeknownst to her mother and sister, she had slipped off and found her dream wedding dress that

6

was a perfect fit for an excellent price. She even put down a deposit; it was just what she saw herself walking down the aisle in to marry him.

*

"That sounds great, baby," said Justin. "I'm happy you found your dress. I'm not going to lie; I was getting a little anxious with the wedding being just a few weeks away." Justin held his hand up, attempting to stop the woman who was trying desperately to undress him while his fiancée was talking nonstop, excitedly.

"Justin, are you all right? You seem preoccupied."

"I'm good, baby."

"Okay, I'll see you tonight," stated Ryane softly.

"Sure, if this storm doesn't lighten up."

"It is bad out. Mother and I barely made it in with the dress before the downpour. I hope Rena stays wherever she is until it stops. She said she had an errand to run."

Oh she did all right…trying to get him in bed, he thought as booming claps of thunder and streaks of lightning startled them both.

"Was that thunder? Oh, Justin, we'll have to see each other tomorrow if this keeps up." Another loud crash accompanied with bolting lightning flashes flickered through her picture window. "Ooh we better hang up, sweetie. I love you."

"Me too," he said, hating himself. After he disconnected the cell, he turned to the woman who had straddled his lap. He knew he couldn't send her out in the storm, but he was not going to surrender to her theatrics. She got him the last time, but he felt much stronger now.

"No, Rena, we can't. I won't. I'm engaged to your sister." He moved her off his lap.

"But you know you love me, Justin."

He'd never admit it, but she was right; he loved them both. He didn't know how or when it happened, but it did. How could that be with them being totally different in some ways but then just alike in others? Nonetheless, he had no intentions of breaking Ryane's heart and embarrassing their families or the church for that matter. Why did he allow things to get out of hand? He knew the answer to his dumb question right off the top…his weak flesh.

"Justin, why can't we? Just this last time, please." She knew if she could make love to him once more, she would have him and began disrobing exposing her shapely legs and thighs.

"No Rena, I mean it," he barked. "Now pull your dress down, and let's find something on television to wait the storm out." The expression on his face made it clear he was not going to allow her to get away with seducing him this time.

*

The big day was drawing nearer, and everything was going according to schedule. Ryane and Justin were beaming with happiness, anticipating their new life as husband and wife.

A rumor had infiltrated throughout the church family which they found to be true. Their minister was retiring from the pulpit, his assistant would take his place, and Justin would become the assistant minister. To add to that good news, their new house was ready and now they could start moving his furniture in along with the pieces they were going to purchase. Ryane was truly happy about that, because her small apartment was already stuffed with wedding gifts, and she still had another bridal shower before the wedding…

Rena had finally accepted that marriage for her and Justin was not a reality. She had not invited herself to his condo anymore and was keeping her distance, as well. It had been hard for him to resist the temptation the night of the storm, but he did with the grace of God. Once again, Justin's life was filled with peace and harmony. He was certain his relationship with Ryane was on solid ground. He was ready to spend the rest of his life making her happy by being the husband she deserved.

However, Justin knew what happened that night was his fault and couldn't be denied. As quiet as it's kept, he'd allowed Rena to have her way and was ashamed to admit he would always cherish that special time they shared. It was more than just sex. She gave him her most precious gift, her virgin body.

Everything happened so fast. When he first tried to stop her, she pouted. Rena then straddled his lap and moved seductively against him. Unbuttoning his shirt, she began planting moist kisses around his neck and down his bare chest while teasing him unmercifully. She was pulling out all the tricks with him moaning her name continuously. He knew he should have stopped her, but his weak flesh had taken control of his total being. Therefore, he did what any helpless man would have done…pleasured her virgin body completely with them having a night of unadulterated lovemaking. But thanks to much prayer and the needed strength he'd been blessed with, the physical attraction for Rena had slowly faded away. And he had not given that night another thought.

*

"Just stack them on the wall labeled bedroom," said Ryane to Justin. His brother and cousins were also there to help.

The male members of his family had come over to keep him company. They had no idea Justin was going to put them to work. While the women were away at the shower, they had moved in the furniture and set up the major rooms at their new home. One of the bedrooms was being used strictly for storage. At the rate things were going, a second one may have to be used which wouldn't be a problem. Only the master suite and one guest room were furnished, along with the family rooms. The shower, her bridesmaids had given her today was certainly needed, and the gifts she received would be used to complete the rooms. When she opened the first gift, which was from Rena, the theme was obvious. She'd given her a beautiful, expensive set of sheets for their king-size bed, and her aunts got together and bought the bedspread and pillows. She was thankful her sister insisted she make a wish list, of course, with her stamp of approval. You would think she was the younger sister instead of being six years older.

10

They had a wonderful time with everyone having fun at her expense with the bedroom gag gifts. Ryane was truly looking forward to the last shower; the theme was lingerie. She could only imagine what she'd receive; probably some sexy, provocative pieces, no doubt…

"Okay, that's the last one," announced his brother. "Did ya'll bring us something to eat?"

"Yes, Avery," replied his wife, Linda. "It's already on the table waiting for you."

He walked over and kissed his pregnant wife and her protruding stomach.

"See what you have to look forward to, Ryane? The Conners men are so affectionate and thoughtful, said her future sister-in-law, Linda." The other Conners women agreed.

Justin had already walked behind his beautiful future wife, caught her around the waist, and nuzzled her neck. He whispered, "I love you."

She hummed, "I know."

"Oh, please!" exclaimed his sister. "Do that in private."

No one paid attention to Rena, who looked like she could have spit nails, but instead, left in a huff, slamming the door behind her. No one commented one way or the other.

*

"Ryane, I'm telling you, it's not wise to cut your hair with you having less than three weeks before the wedding," uttered her hair stylist. "Besides, you know what your *little big* sister said before she left!"

Everyone laughed, because she was so right. Before leaving for her well woman's exam, Rena had given strict instructions how she wanted Ryane's hair done and to cut only split ends. She could get a haircut after the wedding. She needed the long, curly locks for presentation. And then she was given that same lecture: A lot of black women wished they did have natural hair that hung down their back instead of having to add it in.

"Please put your trust in *moi* and allow me to create a masterpiece."

"Okay, Melinda, work your magic."

CHAPTER TWO

Two weeks before the wedding

"Rena, I can't believe this. We only had that one night." He knew that was a dumb statement to make and the expression on her face agreed with him.

She watched him pace back and forth, holding his head. He looked at her and wanted to beg her to take it back but knew she couldn't. Justin had a gut feeling, that on that night, she'd conceived. Ryane had already warned him that the Perry women are very fertile and usually got pregnant their first time, regardless of birth control. That was fine for them; they were ready and wanted to start a family immediately.

Once again, he gazed down at the beautiful young woman who was seven years his junior. What a terrible mess he's made; either way it went down, someone he loved dearly was going to be hurt. "This is my fault," he said in a defeated voice as tears began to drop.

Her heart broke more for this man she was madly in love with than her own sister.

"No Justin, the blame is all mines. I'm the one who deliberately set out to seduce you and hopefully trap you with a baby that I wanted so badly. During our soul-searching talk the night of the storm, I began to really take a good look at myself. My eyes were opened, and I realized how selfish and obsessed I had become." She turned her back to keep a straight face. When she went in for her routine well woman's exam, the day before, she was given fantastic news. Her OB GYN had informed her she was pregnant. She was thrilled to death and could hardly contain herself. That night they spent together, which she would never forget, she conceived. Talk about a blessing! But she had to hold all of the excitement in and convince him, if no one else, that she felt remorse. Okay, she was sorry her sister was going to be hurt and should have thought about that before she set out to seduce her sister's man. It started out as innocent flirting with one thing leading to another, then *Bam,* she found herself wanting him more and more. "Can you ever find it in your heart to forgive me? That's the only way I'm going to get through this and live without you."

He was now standing with his arms around her. She leaned into his stocky but firm frame. "Yes, I can and have forgiven you. And under no circumstances are you going to live without me.

*

"Dr. Newton, we wanted you to be the first one to know, sir." Ryan Newton looked at his future son-in-law and baby girl, silently praying to God they were not going to utter the words he was dreading to hear.

"Know what, son?" he said as if he didn't already have some strong suspicions. Rena had made it her business to always be in Justin's presence, giving a soft touch with an inviting smile. He had witnessed tender looks between the two of them during family dinners and should have said something then. He knew the signs but ignored his baby girl and Justin. But lately, he had seen a change between them and figured whatever had been going on had ceased. But now, he knew more than likely, these two had done the unmentionable, and their secret was about to unfold.

"Rena is pregnant with my child, and we are going to get married."

Dr. Newton solemnly got up from his desk and walked to the picture window in his office. It was a beautiful spring day, with animated clouds dancing about slowly in the sky…peaceful and serene outside, but a thunderstorm was in full effect inside, with the announcement he just received from these two.

With his back still turned away from them, he said, "What do you two expect me to say at this point? Both of you have already made a selfish decision by sleeping with each other in spite of the people that will be hurt, your sister and your fiancée."

You could hear the disgust and anger in his voice. Ryan Newton turned to face them; Rena was now in Justin's arms sobbing.

"Daddy we didn't mean to," she murmured tearfully.

"Please, Rena, save your *'didn't mean to'* for someone who does not know you."

"Sir—"

He was cut off immediately with a deadly stare; one daughter was getting what she wanted at the expense of the other. One was beaming with happiness while the other would surely experience devastation. What's a father to do?

*

"Mother, it's too late to cry about it now. What's done is done."

"You don't act like you have any remorse or shame whatsoever, Rena," cried Beverly Newton.

"Mother, I'm not heartless. I do have remorse, and I hate what has happened. It's just that I don't have any more tears. I'm sorry for this whole, sordid mess, but there's nothing I can do about it now."

Beverly looked at her beautiful daughter and wondered where she went wrong as a mother. Sure she was spoiled, both of her girls were. Although she preferred saying they were able to enjoy the finer things in life…they were privileged. Yes, that was the word… privileged, she thought as she listened to her youngest's sarcastic remarks.

"If it's the *Lord's will,* I will give you and Daddy your first grandchild."

"The *Lord's will,*" she repeated again, high-pitched, "The *Lord's will.* Rena Devonne Newton, how dare you speak the *Lord's* name in the middle of this mess you and the devil have created? Anyway, how long have you been sneaking around with your sister's fiancé?" While she waited for an answer, she was sure she wasn't going to get, Beverly examined her closely.

"Mother, that's irrelevant; the point is I'm carrying Justin's child. And I'm the one he's marrying."

"I sure hope you're not planning a church wedding?"

"And why not, no one else will know about this but daddy, Ryane, and of course, his parents. Both families are expected in a couple of weeks. There will just be some minor changes and a different bride."

"I just don't understand how you could hurt your sister this way, Rena."

"Mother, I didn't mean to, it just happened. How many times must I say that?"

"Does she know yet?"

"Justin is breaking the news to her now."

Beverly couldn't stand to hear another word nor look at this self-centered daughter she raised another second and went to her room...

Rena Newton was about to embark on a wonderful life...In two weeks, she was going to become Justin Lee Conners's wife, have his beautiful baby in six months, and one day become First Lady at Pilgrim Street COC. Yes, ma'am, at twenty-six, she was getting ready to have a fantastic life with a wonderful man, even if she did seduce and trap him with a pregnancy. Besides, she was the best choice, between the Newton girls, to be on his arm. He needed someone who was sophisticated, fashionable, attractive, and outgoing. Being a people's person was not enough. It was simple her Plain Jane sister, Ryane, did not fit the bill. Humph, whether Justin realized it or not, she was saving him from a dull and disappointing life.

*

"Hi, sweetie, let me save this, and then we can talk." Ryane was working on the last section of the church bulletin, her father's self-help article, when she received Justin's call. She could tell something heavy was on his mind.

Ryane got up from her dual role kitchen table and joined him on the sofa. He was rubbing his temple with such a serious expression on his handsome face. She was truly a lucky woman to have him, she thought, gazing at her engagement ring. In a few days, she would be Mrs. Justin Conners and hopefully, pregnant within the month. They had planned a simple, but elegant wedding at their home church. She had a gorgeous wedding gown, although her sister didn't think so. But it was her dream dress and most importantly, she felt beautiful when she put it on. Ryane couldn't wait for their big day, so he could see for himself.

Justin exhaled loudly and turned to face the woman he claimed to love. Yeah right, evidently his love wasn't deep or strong enough to resist her sister's temptation. And what was appalling was that he actually loved Rena with all her conniving and egotistical ways. No, it wasn't right and yes, what they'd done is despicable, but his feelings were genuinely true. The saddest thing, he couldn't begin to say when it occurred. It just crept up on him without any warning. Regardless to what had happened, a wonderful new life was created. But at that

18

very moment, he was getting ready to hurt the one person who didn't deserve that kind of treatment. Ryane Deneen Newton was the kindest, sweetest person you would ever want to meet and know, as far as he was concerned. She was loving, understanding, and supportive. He prayed to God that one day she could forgive them both for their illicit action.

He was taking full responsibility of this situation, in spite of Rena admitting it was her plan along for him to make love to her. None of this could have happened if he hadn't been a willing partner. What was heartbreaking about the whole sordid mess was that he found the intimacy between him and Rena sensuously exciting. And now he was looking forward to sharing a life with her. But most importantly, dear sweet Ryane did not warrant this kind of anguish. Lord, give me strength, he begged silently as he took her hand.

"Ryane, it's no way to say this gently, nor can I sugar coat what I'm about to reveal." He exhaled and then confessed, "I slept with Rena."

"What did you say?" She knew he couldn't have said what she thought she heard. But his facial expression said she'd heard it right. It was plain to see on his face there was no way he could repeat what was just said. Surely, she didn't expect him to. "Did you say you slept with my sister...my sister?" She spoke barely above a whisper, as if someone else was in the room listening. "How could you?" she cried and covered her face.

He leaned toward Ryane as if he was going to touch her. With all her strength, she slapped him and scooted to the other end of her small sofa, out of his reach. She placed her hands over her heart as if she could hold in the shattering pieces that were swiftly chipping away, bit by bit. The hurt she now felt caused by the two people she loved dearly was horrific. The deceitfulness of her sister and fiancé rendered so much pain and anguish.

"Ryane, I'm so sorry."

For a quick second, she glared at him like the deceitful monster he was and then turned her head. Her precious Justin wouldn't stoop to the level this man had. Her man was a God-fearing Christian. He was being groomed by the elders and the ministers to one day become the minister at Pilgrim Street COC.

He stood and knelt in front of her. "Ryane, I need you to—" The distortion on her face and the wave of her hand stopped him cold.

"Don't say another word," Ryane hissed through tears and clenched teeth.

Together, they'd made the decision to wait until their wedding night before becoming intimate. She was still a virgin, although she would have gladly given herself to him. Once they started dating, he decided to become a minister and insisted they practice celibacy. She would remain a virgin until their wedding night. Really, and the entire time he was having sex with her sister.

"Ryane."

"Save it, Justin." She couldn't stand to hear another word nor did she want to and certainly not any details. Or was he going to tell her the wedding should be postponed? Really, that should've been quite clear. It was over as far as she was concerned. What kind of life could they now have? How in the world could she trust him and with her sister, for goodness sake? No, he didn't have to ever worry about her. After tonight, she didn't care if she never set eyes on him again. Eternity would be too soon.

"Justin, there's nothing else you need to say."

His expression said different.

"Rena is pregnant, and I'm going to marry her," he announced quickly.

A boisterous scream followed by painful cries gushed from the depths of her grief-stricken, agonized soul. How could they do this to her? Deceitful monstrous liars, that's what they were. Now everyone would know her fiancé and sister slept together, and were going to have a baby. What humiliation and treachery! Before she knew it, she was leaping toward him, throwing punches repeatedly with her hands and feet like a crazed person. Bodily wrestling her to the floor, he was able to pin her down. He tried speaking softly, hoping that would calm her down. That only made the situation worse, and the foul language she used along with drowning him with spit was totally out of character for his Ryane. She was out of control.

"Ryane, stop…stop," he yelled as he shook her relentlessly. He held her down until she stopped the spitting, and began to cry. He knew he deserved every lick, but she had to calm down.

Through breathless, heart-wrenching sobs, Ryane managed to scream, "Get the hell off of me! Get out!"

He rolled off, and seconds later, she heard her door close. Ryane no longer had the strength to move and turned away, crying hysterically.

*

"Just break the lock, Ryan, she's in there. Her car is in the driveway," pleaded Beverly Newton.

They had given her more than enough time to be alone. She knew her baby was beyond being upset, she was devastated. Already, she had sent texts announcing to family and friends the cancellation of the wedding. All the phones had been ringing constantly with people wanting to know if it was true. Her grandparents were totally upset.

In just two short weeks before her big day, Ryane was faced with this undeserving horror, thought her mother as she helped her husband. Together, they rammed the door, pulling it completely off the hinges. Crossing the threshold and calling her name, they were met with total darkness.

"Be careful, Bev," he warned. "Ryane, it's Daddy and Mother; please answer us, baby."

Her mother stood still and raised her hand. "Shush, listen." Noises were coming from Ryane's small bedroom.

Her parents rushed in and found her throwing clothes in suitcases.

"Ryane, what are you doing?" asked her mother.

"Mother, please, I know you're not expecting an answer," she said in a trembling voice.

Her father was now by her side and sat on her bed. He then took both of her hands in his and pulled his namesake down to sit beside him.

"Daddy, please don't try to talk me out of leaving." She sniffed. "You know I can't stay here now."

He held her tightly in his arms; her mother joined them. Ryane felt her mother's face pressing against her back and could feel the moisture from her tears. Once again, she let a dam of tears burst free as she took comfort in the closeness of her parents. Father, mother, and daughter held on to each other and rocked side to side.

Finally, the tears stopped; she pulled out of her parent's embrace. "Daddy and Mother, I don't have the strength or courage to face anyone," she whispered. "I just want to disappear. Get lost somewhere."

Her father spoke. "Baby, we understand. But don't you think you need the love, comfort, and support of your family and friends right now?"

What they didn't know was that she had refused to talk to her friend, Jackie, who'd been her best friend since kindergarten. She'd also ignored her cousins' calls, and all of them had been raised together like sisters. She was just too ashamed at the moment.

"And have everybody feeling sorry for me, talking behind my back? No Daddy, it's enough she's pregnant, with them planning to get married. Anyway, she's going to need ya'll more with a baby on the way. Our little community will look and judge her harshly, especially once they find out about the pregnancy."

Her parents stared into the face of this beautiful and wonderful person and felt honored she was a part of their lives. She had always made them proud. Graduating with honors and now the manager of one of the top hotels in Texarkana, their girl had done very well. With all the hurt she was feeling, she was thinking of others, namely her sister.

"Don't get me wrong, she deserves everything she's going to get, but I can't stay here. I know what is done is done and I need to move on and make the best of this mess. But I don't want to set eyes on her, especially right now. The only way I can avoid the both of them is to be far away from Texarkana, Arkansas as soon as possible."

"What about your job? You've worked so hard for that position," said her mother.

"Mother, I've already explained the situation to my boss Mr. Knight, and told him I won't be coming back; he understands. He volunteered to check on his Houston connections in helping me get a job. I told him to contact you with the prospects."

24

"Baby, will you give me a chance to make a call?" pleaded her father. You know Pops has first cousins in Texas. As a matter of fact, Dexter Simpson and his family live in a little small southern town called, Allanville, Texas. It's about sixty miles or so from Houston. You remember Dexter?"

She shook her head yes. They would see them at the Texas Lectureships every year.

"We would feel so much better knowing you're with family, even if they are distant cousins."

"Okay, Daddy, I'll wait. Mother, will you help me pack some more of my clothes? I want to get started before dark."

They both looked at her.

"Ryane, that's a long drive for you to do by yourself at night," exclaimed her mother.

"I'm not in a hurry, and the long trip will give me time to think about what I want to do." Her mother knew there wasn't any need in saying another word. She didn't want to upset Ryane any more than she already was. They had gotten a sneak view of Justin when he left her apartment. He looked like he had been in a fight with a wild cat and lost.

"It will be dark soon. Will you at least consider leaving early in the morning instead?"

25

Ryane looked at both parents. Their facial expressions said, *please for our sake.* "Okay, Mother and Daddy, I'll wait until dawn. But please, I don't want to talk to or see anyone. I want to just leave quietly."

*

"Chancey, just the person I needed to talk to."

"I know what about, Minnie. That grandson of mine is missing in action again."

"Exactly, and I didn't want you to think I was lax on the job, because I do have a young lady in mind."

"Okay."

"But it's going to be a challenge, and I will need your help."

"I'll be more than willing to do my part, Minnie. Just tell me what you want me to do."

"Well, you know your grandson better than anyone, and I can only speculate how to go about this. So I want you to listen to my plan and see if you think it will work.

CHAPTER THREE

"Mother, she's gone! I mean really gone. What about her job? She worked hard for that position." Rena didn't think for one minute Ryane would leave Texarkana or Arkansas, for that matter. Yes, she would be hurt and embarrassed, but with time and the birth of the baby, she would bounce back. She always did. After all, they were more than sisters; she was the closest person she had as a best friend. Yes, she had girlfriends, but no one was like her Ryane. She'd always been there for her in spite of her being a spoiled, selfish brat. It has always been just the two of them with Rena being the boss, regardless of her being the younger sister. "Daddy, you couldn't stop her? What about Grandma and Big Daddy...Nanny and Pawpaw? She could have at least waited."

"Waited for what, Rena? Did you think for one minute your sister was going to stick around and watch you marry?" Her mother stopped because she became emotional. Her baby was alone because of her conniving and unethical sister.

"Go ahead and say it, Mother. I slept with the man she was going to marry, and now I'm pregnant with his baby, your first grandchild." She schemed and plotted to have her sister's man. Not once did she stop to think of the consequences that night; all she knew was how she felt and what she wanted. Sure, she flirted with Justin but it was harmless at first, pretty much just her being a pest.

It was never supposed to be serious. She didn't know when she fell in love with him; it just happened.

Her father now spoke for the two of them in a tone she was not accustomed to at all. "Rena, what you've done is sinful disgusting and plain unspeakable. And yes, your mother and I have been looking forward to being grandparents. But the way you went about giving us our first grandbaby has robbed us of our joy for the moment. I'm sure even you can understand that. Nonetheless, we will be here for you, but forgive us if we're not bubbling over with excitement right now."

Complete silence hung over the room, neither parent spoke. Rena knew she had disappointed them both and sensed their effort to hold back the anger and contempt they had for her. Not once had her father spoken to her in such a manner before, not his baby. Of course, she'd never given him a reason to. Like Ryane, they were daddy's girls and had always done what's right. By no means did they ever want to disappoint or embarrass their wonderful parents.

"And you know what's so ironic about this whole sordid mess, Rena?" exclaimed her mother. "Your sister said you would need us more once the news of what you've done gets out."

She looked at her parents with genuine remorse and real tears. Above a whisper Rena spoke, "Ryane said that?"

Before they could answer with a *Yes*, there was a knock. Her father went to the door; it was their future son-in-law who had been engaged to marry one sister but got the other one pregnant. That's how Ryan Newton felt, although he would never utter the words aloud.

"Dr. Newton."

"Justin, everyone is in the family room." Dr. Ryan Newton turned to lead the way. His wife was right; he did look like he had been in a fight and lost. Justin followed and was grateful they were all together, especially thankful that Ryane was with her parents. He had knocked on her door first but did not get an answer. When he left her yesterday, she was in a hysterical state, which was well understood. Now, with them all together, he could apologize and beg their forgiveness without Ryane becoming violent.

"Oh Justin," Rena paused in shock. "What happened to you? Your face," she said, lightly touching a badly scratched and bruised cheek. He even had a black eye.
"Don't concern yourself with my face. I'm all right, what about Ryane?"

"Ryane is gone. She's packed up and left." Rena snuggled in his arms, crying, with him displaying confusion and shock.

"Baby, what are you saying?"

Her mother answered for her. "Ryane is no longer here, and I don't know when I'll see my baby." She too began to cry, with her husband consoling her. That scene tore at Justin's heart, because the whole sleazy ordeal was

29

his fault. He could never erase the hurt and pain, let alone the embarrassment he'd inflicted. That was one thing his parents had made perfectly clear. They also emphasized that he was just as selfish and self-absorbed, along with a few other choice adjectives, as Rena, and they both deserved each other.

With raw emotions, Justin began, "Dr. and Sis. Newton, I want to say how deeply sorry I am, and I'm taking full responsibility for the entire situation. I hope and pray that both of you will find it in your hearts to forgive me."

"Son, it's our Christian duty to do so, first of all; therefore, you are forgiven. Secondly, you're still going to be a member of this family, and we won't be your problem. Rest assured, be not fooled, you and Rena will encounter strong oppositions for a while. Besides making a lot of people unhappy, needless to say, your behavior has been very disappointing."

Justin took out his handkerchief and wiped his face.

"Now, when do you two plan to get married?"

"Daddy, we can keep the date Ryane had. All the arrangements have been made and paid for."

So she still doesn't have a clue, thought her mother who began to lay everything out in the open. "First of all, young lady, all has been cancelled by Ryane and confirmed by us. Secondly, you will have a closed, simple ceremony here with immediate family only. Your father and I, Justin's parents, his two siblings, and grandparents of course, will be in attendance. That's it! Furthermore, I

30

will advise you two to get your licenses as soon as possible.   And foremost, you will not get married on the day Ryane had chosen. Let me suggest Tuesday around noon; that should give you plenty of time to get any and everything else needed for your day. Oh, and Rena, please find a dress that's appropriate. Justin, here's Ryane's engagement ring plus the other trinkets. Maybe you can salvage the ring for Rena." What she was thinking she kept to herself. She wanted her sister's fiancé; she may as well have the rest of the things he'd given her. Beverly Newton had spoken, and Rena knew it was best to do exactly what had been suggested.

"Okay, Mother."

"Justin?"

"Certainly, Sis. Newton," he said.

"All right, your father and I will take care of the details and naturally, foot the bill."

"Thank you, Mother and Daddy," she said softly.

"Are there any other concerns?" asked her father as he looked from one to the other.

They both whispered no.

*

"Mother, I'm finally here and so far, from what I've seen, Allanville is a wonderful little country town. Before I forget, Uncle Dexter and Aunt Minerva said hello."

31

Her mother smiled at the title uncle and aunt. Although they were distant cousins, she knew it was their way of making her feel like close family. Ryane's tone said they had accomplished just that.

"Baby, I'm so glad you made it safely, and tell them I said, hello. So do you think you're going to like it there?"

"Yes, Mother, I am; anywhere is better than home." She spoke before thinking. "Oh, Mother, I didn't mean—"

Her mother stopped her because she knew what she meant.

"I've already talked to daddy. He said he and the elders are having a meeting with Justin at his request."

"Yes, baby, they're meeting as we speak."

"Well, whatever. I hope he and my sister are very happy. Now Mother, some good news, I may have a job at the new hotel they have here. Uncle Dexter's nephew is going to speak with one of the proprietors. I'll keep you and Daddy posted. Oh, dinner is ready; I'll call you before I go to bed. Bye, Mother, I love you."

"Mother loves you, too, precious." Beverly could still hear the sadness in her baby's voice, which was expected, but she felt confident that she would be all right. Her Ryane always bounced back. But she didn't know about Ms. Rena.

CHAPTER FOUR

Ryane's suitcases were finally unpacked with everything put in its proper place in the small two bedroom cottage that she would now call home. It was next door to her new aunt and uncle. It once belonged to his sister, who never married, and now Ryane was welcomed to live in it as long as she wanted to. She even had a porch that she could sit on to enjoy the fresh, country air. Ryane waved to her new family as she took a seat to drink her tea in the rocker she bought yesterday. They had been absolutely wonderful. It was just that the pain and hurt was still there. She needed to answer her text messages, but she couldn't bring herself to, including Jackie's and her cousin Darlene's. The only people she'd communicated with were her parents and grandparents. She just couldn't right now.

In the meantime, she'd met a new friend, Shelly Roberts, even though she was a few years younger than herself. Her aunt's niece, Shelly, had been a jewel by making her feel welcome. They'd spent the last couple of days transforming the cottage into a lovely home, stocking her place with needed supplies, since she'd come with only her clothes and personal items. It took two trips to the strip mall to purchase what she needed and wanted. Finally, she had her new place exactly like she fancied with the help of her new found friend. She now had a lovely little country house with a great, landscaped yard.

Now that her home was done, it was time to take care of Ryane. She wanted a new look to go along with a new job she was claiming. When she mentioned she wanted her hair cut into a new style, Shelly offered to introduce her to her hairstylist, LaRhonda. Ryane's *cell* rang, *it was* her cousin, Vic.

"Ryane, this is Vic. I've set up an interview at the hotel for you Tuesday at twelve noon with Mr. McGowan."

"OMG, so soon?"

"Yes, Ryane, you came at the right time, and I do have connections. The hotel is in need of an experienced executive manager. I passed your name to the main man, the judge. So, babygirl come to impress." He spent a few minutes giving her some little tidbits he thought would be helpful.

When Ryane disconnected, all she could think about was her prayers had been answered.

According to her Uncle Dexter, the hotel would be a wonderful place for employment. It was a beautiful, newly constructed business and a popular spot in their little town which they were very proud of. When she asked about Judge McGowan, her uncle said he was retired and a fair man. She didn't need to worry. Uncle Dexter had also shared the history of his town with pride and admiration.

The predominately black, country town was once a huge farm and cattle ranch owned by Allan Parker. In the late fifties, he sold the land to a group of black, World War II veterans who were small farmers and ranchers, along

34

with a few entrepreneurs. A town was developed, which now boasted a population of over eleven thousand with sixty-five percent of those residents being African Americans. Allanville, Texas was an ideal town to raise a family in and was constantly growing. Because of a little farming, ranching, normal town businesses, and the railroad system, the town's economy flourished. In addition to three major companies and a new penal transfer facility in one of the neighboring towns, there were excellent job opportunities available. Some of the young people who grew up in the small town had returned with their own families to take over family businesses, while others had started new ones. But for the most part, the simple, easy living and low crime rate had attracted many, especially retirees. And now, she was making it her home.

*

LaRhonda turned Ryane around in the chair so she could see how she looked. She was amazed, to say the least, and very pleased. Ryane has gotten that new haircut she'd wanted for so long. She now had a totally new look, nothing like the old Ryane, and that was a good thing. She needed the look to accompany her new mindset, *you won't get to do me*, she thought as she admired her reflection in the mirror. The short, asymmetric cut was chic and becoming.

"Well, what cha' think?"

"I love it, LaRhonda, especially the golden highlights." Her cell chimed, it was her mother. "Excuse me for a minute. Hi Mother."

"Ryane, it's me."

"What are you doing with Mother's cell? Better yet, what do you want?"

With the nasty tone she used Rena should have hung up, but she couldn't and didn't. She wanted to hear her sister's voice but without the venomous hostility, although she deserved it.

"Ryane, please, I'm sorry, and I need you to say you forgive me."

"Why should I Rena, because you're my spoiled *azz* selfish and immoral sister?!"

Rena began to cry.

"Really Rena, keep the tears for someone who cares, because I certainly don't give a damn."

"Ryane, I regret terribly what I've done. How long are you going to stay mad at me?"

"Eternity wouldn't be too soon," she said between tight lips. "So please don't call me again, because there's nothing for us to talk about, ever. Now you and Justin have a great life, and leave me the hell alone." She swiped her cell before she put it back in her purse, and calmly said, "I'm sorry about." Ryane then picked up the mirror to see the back of her hair like nothing had happened.

The two ladies did the same, turning their attention to her, waiting for her reaction. Once again, she was pleased. She looked at the stylist and then her cousin. "What do you think?"

"Oh, Ryane, I love it," exclaimed her new friend,

Shelly. "But girl, you were brave to cut all that hair at one time."

Ryane said thank you while looking at Shelly's bold, dark-brown and honey blonde streaked Mohawk, which blended perfectly with her honey-colored complexion. She was a gorgeous, bodacious, twenty-nine-year-old, six foot, plus-size woman who could not be ignored. Men were always approaching her, and she thought nothing of it. Ryane didn't understand why she wasn't married; her criteria list for a husband must be steep.

Shelly gave a hearty laugh. "Girl, I know, how can I talk?"

Ryane laughed along with her.

"Okay girlfriend, you need to get back to the house to get ready for that interview, and I'll see you afterwards and we can have lunch to celebrate."

"Are you counting your chickens before they hatch?"

"No *Dear-Dear,* just being positive and confident," laughed Shelly.

"Okay, I'll call when it's over."

"You won't have to," she said, going to the door.

"I won't have to," Ryane called out as she unzipped her designer bag. But Shelly was already out of the salon. She paid LaRhonda with a generous tip and left.

*

"Rena, are you ready? Everyone is here." Beverly

knocked, then entered her daughter's room.

She was staring in the full length mirror.

"Oh, baby, you look so pretty."

She closed her eyes to fight back the tears. Rena didn't think her mother would ever refer to her as baby again. She knew the shame she'd brought upon her family. That was why she wasn't having the wedding of her dreams and had no one to blame but herself.

Beverly turned her beautiful daughter around to kiss her cheek and place her corsage of lilac and pink flowers with a cream ribbon on her left wrist.

"Thank you, Mother. It's perfect." Rena was moved; her mother had it made with her favorite colors.

"You're welcome, baby." Her mother couldn't believe she'd had Melinda to cut all her hair off. That was Ms. Rena's pride and joy. But Beverly guessed she wanted a complete change and a new identity. Whichever was the case, the new style was very becoming, just like the soft satin, A-line dress she chose. The strapless, tea-length column gown in cream with a pearl broach was perfect for her petite frame and new look. Open-toed pumps and her borrowed diamond jewelry were her accessories.

"Oh, Mother, I'm so sorry about what I've done. I wish I could undo it all, regardless of how much I love him, but that's not possible. Do you think Ryane will ever forgive me?"

"Of course she will one day. But right now, she's hurting something awful."

Rena dared not tell her mother she used her cell to call Ryane that morning to ask for her forgiveness, which had been a total disaster. Her sister was beyond hurt, she was angry and bitter. And she now had to accept that fact because of her deception. Ryane was different. She was no longer the sweet, gentle, loving, big sister when it came to her. But that wouldn't stop Rena's constant prayer that one day their relationship would be restored.

"Come on, Justin is waiting for you."

Her father met them in the hall way. "You look pretty, baby."

She couldn't contain her tears any longer and fell upon her father's shoulder. He patted her like he'd always done when she came crying to him for whatever reason. He knew she was unhappy. Her mother told him she called Ryane, but used her cell. No doubt, that didn't work out well at all, which was understood.

"Okay, that's enough. Bev, take her back and fix those black tears. My babygirl is not a panda bear."

That put a smile on her face, and they returned to her room to do just that. A few minutes later, they were back. Her parents escorted her to their large family room where invited family members waited. Her face showed how surprised she was to see the room beautifully decorated in her favorite colors, as she walked toward the love of her life. He was handsomely dressed in a suit that was a darker shade in the champagne color spectrum.

He took her in his arms and whispered, "You look beautiful, baby," and kissed her cheek. The minister began.

*

"Ryane, you've come highly recommended by two people I have great respect for, and I don't see a reason to prolong this interview," said Chancey McGowan, Jr. What he didn't say was that Minnie was right. She was perfect for his grandson. Yes, they'd come up with a great plan to bring the two together. He knew why she had relocated, which said a lot for her character. She chose to count her loses, pick herself up, leave everything behind, and start fresh. That was the attitude of a strong, determined black woman. He knew with those qualities, her head would not be turned because of good looks and smooth words. She would be a challenge, and his grandson was one who thrived on meeting them head on. He took great pleasure, and always had, in doing what was said to be off limits. *Ms. Newton is ideal for him, and he's man enough to make her forget the pain she's endured and give true love a real chance.* "How are your chops?"

"Tender and juicy, just like I like them," she said, trying to remember this was an interview in spite of her connections. Talk about a blessing. He and her old boss Mr. Knight were army buddies, and attended PVU when it was known as Prairie View A&M College.

"Good, now the job is yours if this salary is acceptable." He dabbed at his mouth and then wrote down his offer and handed it to her.

Only five thousand less than her old salary, she wasn't expecting the small town hotel to pay her anything close to what he offered, even if it was a fabulous place. "Yes Mr. McGowan, this is acceptable," she said with a smile.

40

"Very good, Ms Newton; we look forward to working with you. When can you start?"

"Now, sir, and thank you for this opportunity," Ryane said.

His snippy smile said she made the right decision. "One other thing," he said, giving her a binder. "Everything you need to know about our town and the hotel is in this along with the zip drive. I know how you young people prefer these technology toys. Please familiarize yourself with all the information so you can become a proud *Allanvilleian*. Are there any questions?"

"No, Sir.

"Fine, welcome to our community and family," he replied and signaled for his personal assistant and driver. "Mr. Anderson, will you show Ms. Newton to Human Resources and have Ms. Roberts show her around."

"Of course Judge, Ms. Newton," said her cousin, Vic.

"Good bye Sir," Ryane said, trying to hold in her surprise.

Vic winked and took her arm.

She texted her mother to let her know she got the job and would give her details later. She knew they were busy; today Rena was marrying her ex.

*

"Thank you, Daddy and Mother, for everything. Considering the circumstances, you two have made this a wonderful day."

They both expressed it was their pleasure and she was quite welcome.

Still lingering looking around the room as if her sister was going to appear, she said she would see them in a few days. Her mother embraced her and whispered it was going to get better. Her father took her arm; they walked to the front door where her husband stood. Justin also thanked her parents, and then took his beautiful bride's hand.

He kissed her before she got in the car and reemphasized how much he loved her new look. She was pleased and told him she was glad. For a honeymoon, they were going to a historical, black owned bed and breakfast inn located on the outskirts of Little Rock, AR, Ms. Tilley's. It was a gift from both of his grandparents.

"Your parents did a fantastic job in spite of the situation we put them in."

"Yes, they did, and I expressed those very sentiments along with how appreciative we were."

He gave her hand a gentle squeeze.

Rena smiled, because she knew he was as surprised as she was when they saw the elaborate arrangement her parents had provided. Their great room had been transformed into an elegant, small banquet room for the ceremony and dinner. Round tables and chairs were covered in cream linen topped with sheer scarves and sashes of her favorite colors. For centerpieces, short vases filled with bouquets of lilac and pink roses sat on mirrors. The tables were also graced with complete place settings of fine china for each guest. A potted tree from the back patio decorated with satin bulbs in the same pastel colors and tied with cream ribbon sat in the center of the room. That was where they stood to repeat their vows. What was touching was the unity sand ceremony. Three mason jars labeled *his, hers*, and *ours* sat on the mantle with cream ribbon tied around them. *His* and *hers* had sand which they poured into the one labeled *ours* after they completed their vows. A delicious dinner of roasted chicken and her favorite pork chops with sides were catered and served. They even had a one-layer wedding cake with vanilla ice cream, another favorite. In spite of all the anguish she'd caused, her parents still came through, giving her a day she'd cherish always.

CHAPTER FIVE

"Okay Shelly, tell me the truth. You knew the job was in the bag from the beginning."

"Girl, it pays to have connections." She laughed and took a bite of the grilled fish she'd ordered. Not only was Victor Judge McGowan's personal assistant, Shelly worked in the human resource department. Not one time had jobs come up in any of their conversations. With Shelly and Vic in her corner, she couldn't help but get the job. Ryane knew then she had truly found a real friend, and life was not going to be so lonely in Allanville, after all. "How you like that salary?"

"Girl, I was shocked when I saw all those numbers and zeroes."

"I'll tell you this much, you had some serious competition, but your experience is what actually sealed the job. Don't be fooled by the Judge, he doesn't care who you know or what your last name is. You can ask some of his nieces and nephews that. None of them have made manager or department head yet."

"Really," commented Ryane.

"Yes, ma'am, whose position do you think you're replacing?" She didn't give Ryane the chance to attempt to answer. "The Judge's brother's son, who wasn't qualified, but he thought because of his last name it was a done deal. But all in all, you're going to love working at the inn and you have a great group of employees."

"I'm glad to hear that, because I have some wonderful ideas and suggestions that I have in mind. And the Judge has already said it was my show."

"You go girl, he likes you."

"And you too, I noticed."

"According to my *Dear-Dear,* I resemble his wife, who was a big woman."

"He's one handsome old dude himself," said Ryane.

"You can say that again."

She did with them bursting into laughter; both acknowledging silently they were glad they'd met and were now friends.

"I'm thirsty, let's go to the lounge," Shelly suggested.

Ryane hadn't had any liquor since her freshman year in college, and that was a terrible experience then. She liked Shelly, and they had hit it off great, but she knew she may as well tell her she was not into hard liquor. "Shelly, I don't drink alcohol."

"Girl, who said anything about liquor? Besides, Allanville is in a dry county." Shelly shook her head and told her to come on.

Just down a piece, they entered the supposed-to-be lounge. Shelly introduced her as the hotel's new executive manager and ordered their drinks. They sat at one of the Bistro tables where they could watch the patrons enter the nice-sized room. The waitress brought their fruit smoothies, which were delicious.

"So Shelly, I'm really replacing one of his nephews."

"Yes, ma'am. And you'll get to meet him. He's handsome, as well. Humph, all of the Judge's nephews are good looking, but none of them compare to his oldest, drop dead gorgeous grandson that's fine to the bone and his namesake. Mr. Chancey Renard McGowan, IV, better known as Chocolate Swirl, *babie*...when that man enters a room you know it, because time actually stands still."

"Really, Shelly, is he that fine or are you exaggerating a bit?"

"Let me put it this way, he has all the women dripping and drooling, wanting to lick some chocolate up and down."

"Dripping, what do... auh...Shelly Roberts, you're just plain despicable."

"No, just a twenty-eight-year-old sister soon to be a year older, who's horny, so stone me to death," she said and sipped her drink.

Ryane looked at her for a second and they both broke into teenage giggles.

"With that personality of yours, why don't you approach him?"

"I have, but he wasn't interested and didn't hesitate to let me know, too. I figured he probably had two reasons, my last name and he's not into big women. Then too, I've never heard of him being with any of the Allanville sisters, which made me feel better and was a comfort to my ego.

He's a *bonified player playa* with big bucks. Girl, he's so fine, I've heard women pay for one night with Mr. McGowan. Of course, that's hearsay. I don't know anybody personally who has done such. Yours truly has thought about driving right to where he works and solicit his services." She heard Ryane gasp. "I know I'm despicable."

"No, you're honest and real. I like that."

"I don't know any other way, Ryane. So please put me in my place or just say, 'Mind your own business Shelly, with what I'm about to ask. If I may be so bold, what was that all about back at the salon?"

Ryane looked at her and then looked away. She knew that was going to come up, because she didn't try to conceal her feelings concerning the person she was talking to and knew it was obvious it was her sister. With the second round of drinks, she told her new friend the entire, sordid mess. Shelly was very sympathetic but told her she couldn't ward off men just yet. She had the rest of her life ahead of her and just hadn't met the right one. Ryane could tell she was speaking from experience.

Shelly had her heart broken when she was only eighteen. She met her first and only love during her senior year in high school. They even enrolled in PVU together. But she found out his agenda was totally different from hers. He was ready to take their relationship to another level and have sex, but she wasn't ready for that gigantic step at the time. He didn't want to wait, so they broke up. She often wondered, after they went their separate ways, whether he loved her or not. Was he just trying to add another virgin to his repertoire? At any rate, he eventually quit school, and she hadn't heard from him since.

47

Periodically, she'd run into some of his family, since they live in Allanville, and asked about him. In the beginning, they were so vague when it came to him and his whereabouts that she finally quit asking. Later, she heard he was making a career out of the service and had married one of the local women where he was stationed and now has two kids.

After they finished bonding more with their broken hearted stories, Shelly filled her in on her administrative teams and some of the workers. She reemphasized that the hotel had a great group of employees. And like she said before, if troubles arise, it would be some of the young McGowan clan. Ryane mentally thought she wouldn't have a problem putting them in their places. This was her hotel now.

"Well, Boss Lady, I must return to my office."

"That's right, I am *The Boss*, the one in charge," she squealed. "Thank you, Shelly."

"Ms. Newton, like I said before and I meant what I said, it was your credentials that sealed the deal."

The new friends and coworkers embraced and said their good byes. Ryane then got comfortable and took out her tablet to make notes. The lounge was an area she could address immediately at a reasonable cost. With that in mind, she began putting her suggestions for changes down...

Although the lounge had only a few customers, no one noticed the dark, handsome man who quietly entered the area through the staff's entrance. He took a seat in the back to get a good look at the new manager and came to the conclusion that the judge did all right this time. He had checked her out, and Ryane Newton came with some highly impressive qualifications. She was as smart as she was beautiful, with her inviting smile. He studied her closely and noticed several times that she reached for a curly lock she no longer had. He looked at her profile on his cell and couldn't believe she cut all that gorgeous hair, but she now possessed a sexy sassiness with her new style. Justin Conners must have been a damn fool to let her slip away. Surely he hadn't tapped that curvaceous and voluptuous body. If he hadn't, no way should he have allowed her to get away until he did so. Chancey McGowan pulled up her sister's profile. Okay, she was cute and her curves were nice, but she didn't compare to her big sister. He loved his women thick and babygirl was *sho dat*. Chancey caressed the hairs on his chin and silently said he was definitely going to tap that *azz*. But right now, he needed some undisturbed rest, and then he would come up with a game plan. It was certain he was going to have to use his real slick moves on Ms. Ryane Newton. She was no pushover, especially after being dumped by her fiancé for her little sister. Man, that was what you call some deep *chitilians* and babygirl had to be dealing with some serious pain and trust issues. With a big grin, the perfect plan came to mind. But later, Rocky, he said silently to his twitching manhood and disappeared as discreetly as he appeared...

Ryane completed her task and packed her things to call it an evening. She decided Friday night was when her plan would go into effect. All that was needed was notification to the managers to pass the word to their team. She would consult with the hotel's fabulous chef to suggest a simple menu that would be easy to prepare and restock. They could also use satellite music for the time being, unless someone on staff had DJ experience. She said good night and left for the night.

CHAPTER SIX

"Hi, Mother, I finally got a break to call you back." It had been hectic those last few days, trying to get things in order at the job and the cottage.

"Hi, Ryane, so the job is working out fine? Have you moved into your office, yet? How big is it? Have you personalized it, yet? What about the cottage? I bet it's adorable."

"Mother, slow down; by the end of the week you'll have lots of pictures showing off the cottage and my office. As we speak, I'm sitting on one of the benches located in one of their beautiful gardens just outside my office. I had my first meeting with the managers yesterday, and today I met with the different departments. Everyone has been friendly and helpful."

"Sounds wonderful Ryane, and you seem to be adjusting fine."

"Let's say I have something to keep me busy that I enjoy and love doing. Besides, I have to move on with my life and not feel sorry for myself, any longer." There was silence for a few seconds. "I guess Rena and Justin are happy, now; they got what they wanted," she said with cold bitterness.

"Ryane, I know you're still hurt."

She interrupted her, "No, Mother, I'm over the hurt. I'm mad as hell, but I will be okay."

"Baby, please don't allow anger and bitterness to consume you. It's not healthy. You're young and have your whole life ahead of you. Someone else will come along that—"

Ryane interrupted her. "Mother, please, let's not go into that again. I can't believe you would even utter those words to me. With no disrespect, that was a waste of energy and time. I will never trust another woman's son... and certainly not love one...and that's a promise." Ryane was quiet for a second. "Mother, I'm going to have to talk to you later. I want to check on a few things. It will probably be too late when I get in, so I'll call you sometime tomorrow. And Mother, please don't worry about me, really, I'm going to be just fine. Love you, and tell Daddy I said hello."

Beverly Newton's aching heart broke in half at hearing her daughter's new revelation. Thirty-two was too young for any healthy female to give up on love, especially a vibrant, beautiful, and wonderful woman like her Ryane. And she knew that was exactly the mind-set of her determined baby. It was going to take a strong, hardnosed man to chip away that concrete interior.

Ryane picked up her bag and went to her car. She was going to take a nice shower and change clothes. She and Shelly were going to hang out in the inn's lounge tonight along with some of the other younger employees to help boost the new changes. *Boss Lady* didn't see any reason to wait to implement her ideas to attract more of the locals. Furthermore, she needed to do something to occupy her mind instead of crying over what was supposed to have happened this weekend—tonight, her bachelorette party and tomorrow, her wedding. But thanks to betrayal

and deception, that event was null and void…over with…
cancelled out…done.

*

"Yes Judge, his *Cayenne* is back in the driveway in
the exact same spot."

Instead of staying at the hotel for the last couple of
days, Chancey opted to spend his time at his
grandparent's house. He was that tired and needed the
rest. No one had seen him, including the cook. The Judge
gathered he would eat whenever he caught up on his rest.
It wasn't unusual for him to hide out at the house after
taking care of some of his so-called business.

"Thanks, Vic; I'll see you in the morning."

"You're welcome, Judge; good night."

Judge McGowan retired to his living quarters for the
night. Sometimes, his grandson would stay away for weeks
doing Lord knows what. As long as he was in the armed
forces, the Judge knew he was fine. After eighteen years,
he decided to retire from the Air Force, but remained in the
Reserve. Nevertheless, his life has gone downhill as far as
the Judge was concerned. Although he'd never had any
run-ins with the law, his business ethics were questionable.
With the elaborate lifestyle he was living, whatever he was
involved in couldn't be all legit, although his father had
checked him out thoroughly. Supposedly, he worked in
that fancy hotel in Houston. Lord only knows doing what,
with a nickname *Chocolate Swirl*. He claimed he was a
certified bartender and had an investment in a promotion
company. Chancey Jr. couldn't imagine somebody with
his grandson's credentials and education holding down a

job making drinks. He'd heard stories concerning other activities but didn't know how true they were. Whatever he was doing had to be shady for him to drive an expensive vehicle and wear the best designer-wear money can buy. He spent more money on a pair of shoes than he did for a suit, and they were far from being cheap. It was a known fact that a large portion of the trust fund his mother's grandparents set aside for him was invested in Allanville's hotel, and the remainder was probably depleted by now unless he'd made some additional investments, only HE knew.

The Judge knew he raised his oldest grandson with a stern, harsh hand, but it was necessary. He didn't want to lose him to the streets. That was the purpose of taking full responsibility of guardianship since his parents were only sixteen and the mother's family didn't want the responsibility of raising a baby at their age. On the other hand, the Judge and his wife didn't hesitate to take their grandson. After all, his father was their only child and had his whole life ahead of him, college and law school. He and his wonderful wife were sure they were doing the right thing at the time by raising him as their own. Nevertheless, Chancey was brought up in a fine and loving home with a strong foundation; whatever happened now is on him. If he didn't change his ways and settle down, he would be forced to make some changes in his will. Ryane Newton was his last hope…

Chancey was dressed as his usual savvy self for the night, but he thought he would spend a few minutes with the old man. He heard him when he closed his room door. His stomach growled which was a reminder; he hadn't eaten in twenty-four hours. He'd get something at the hotel while he checked Ms. Newton out up close, he thought as he knocked on his grandfather's door. He received a grumpy, "Come in," and entered.

"Hi, Pops."

"Son, so you decided to finally join the living?"

"Yep, Judge, I was in need of a much-deserved rest. So, how are you enjoying retirement? Are you keeping yourself busy? You have a girlfriend, yet?"

"My retirement is great, and yes, I'm keeping myself busy, and I won't dignify that last ridiculous question with an answer. Nonetheless, it's good to see you. How long has it been?"

Chancey knew he hadn't been home since his grandfather's big retirement party, and that was five weeks ago, but that's how his business worked. "It's been a minute Grandfather, but I'll be here for a spell." His plans were to be around for a while, and in the meantime, romance the new hotel manager his grandfather hired while he was in town. Chancey tried to visit the old man as often as he could to make sure he was following doctor's orders, especially since the little scare with his heart. And at the same time, he got the opportunity to enjoy the small town's easy, slow pace and tranquility. Between the Reserve and the hectic life he lived in Houston, his time in Allanville was drama free with total relaxation. That was why he did not get involved with the local females. His personal rule: they were off limits. They had two things on their minds...marriage and babies, which was not in his repertoire for the moment. His line of work made it too complicated to get involved in a serious relationship, and a family was out of the question. His big city living enabled him to have adult fun with selective, sophisticated, career-minded beauties who thought like him...*no strings attached.* That was the thing about Chancey McGowan; he was not a one-woman man. He was definitely a member of the *players' playa* club. "I'm outta here. I just stopped in to holler."

"Where are you off to?"

"I thought I would have dinner at the hotel and meet the new hotel manager."

"Ms. Newton is off limits. Consider her a native Allanvilleian." A smile spread across their faces for different reasons.

"See you in the A.M., Grandfather."

Chancey Jr. knew he had issued a challenge that his grandson had no intentions of passing up. Yep, the old man still had it, he thought with a smile on his face as he listened to his namesake leave the house.

CHAPTER SEVEN

It was Friday night and this time the hotel's parking lot was packed. Although Ryane had been employed with the hotel for only a few days, tonight was special. The first new change implemented by her was in full gear. As she pulled into her designated parking spot she saw Shelly in the hotel window. Once inside she was greeted by Shelly and the rest of the staff.

"Wow, Boss Lady, you look fabulous," Shelly said cheerfully.

"And let me return the compliment."

The new friends had the same idea in mind: black party dresses to flaunt their sexiness while exposing ample curves, shapely healthy thighs, and legs. Both dresses complemented their individual, sassy boldness. Ryane's was a satin, layered, sleeveless trapeze float with a beaded neckline which highlighted her nice shoulders. Shelly's hand-beaded, detailed one-shoulder strapped dress had deep magenta florals and a short, flirty tail. Both wore large, bold earrings and strappy sandals, which made their look super sexy.

The ladies walked down the short corridor in the lobby to their destination. Although they could not hear that a party was going, they knew so. The parking lot was full. As they approached the newly installed soundproof doors, the music and party cheers could barely be heard, that was the main idea. Ryane was quite pleased with the picture she envisioned when she opened them. Her idea was right on the money. And before she was done, this little spot was also going to be an enhancement for local entertainment. The small town hotel would now offer what the larger cities did, a cocktail lounge during the day and for the grown and sexy, an elegant upscale lounge club after dark with a dress code. They would not only attract their guests but the local residents who wanted to dress to impress, enjoy a nice, delicious spread and music to set the mood for some neighborly socializing and mingling. And that was exactly what she observed when she spotted Vic. He waved them over to his table, which was in the midst of the crowd. She could see all around the room, including the entrance. With the new arrangement of the Bistro table sets, they were able to add additional décor along with a couple of loveseats. The atmosphere was laid-back and pleasurable.

"Ladies, don't you look gorgeous," exclaimed Vic.

They also received a nod and an appreciative smile from his two male guests who had already visited the steam table. They told them thank you while looking around the room.

"You have a happy crowd, as you can see. Girl, you did this." His table guests agreed while they enjoyed their refreshments.

"Well thank you, cuz. I believe I'll move around a bit and listen to the buzz. Shelly, you want to join me?"

"Only if we go in the direction of the buffet table, I'm starved."

"Girlfriend, you read my mind." Shelly smiled and

the two friends excused themselves.

Once they were out of earshot, Jarvis asked, "Man, why didn't you introduce us to the ladies. *Ooowee*, look how those dresses are *swanging* on their luscious behinds."

"Watch your mouth, man, and that's why. Anyway, you already know my cousin, Shelly, and the other lady Ryane, is a distant cousin from Arkansas. She's also the executive hotel manager, definitely out of your league."

"What's that supposed to mean?"

"You don't cut the mustard, dumbbell," replied his friend, Marcus.

"Why, because I'm a manual laborer who has to get dirty to do his job?"

"Naw, man, because you're ignorant," said Vic laughing. "But we love you just the same."

"At least I don't play nurse maid to the judge," said Jarvis snidely.

"Personal assistant, there's a difference. And Jarvis, man, you don't make the kind of money I make in two weeks during your best month," boasted Vic.

"Dang man, can you hook a brother up?" asked Marcus.

Vic looked at him to see if he was serious. "Doing what, man? The Judge doesn't need any help. His staff is complete. Now, the hotel is a different story; they'll have some openings soon with this new manager. So, look intelligent and impress the lady. And Jarvis, I'm warning you stay away from my cousins."

Ryane felt a sense of pride with the success of her first project, as she walked around the room to visit the guests. Shelly had fixed her a plate and returned to Vic's table. Ryane couldn't help herself and began to assist the steam table assistant. The presentation was enticing and quite appetizing with the guests taking advantage of the free food. Most of the crowd was between twenty-five to about forty, give or take a few years. Although the prices of the drinks had been raised, no one seemed to mind with the tasty cuisine offered.

The same wonderful sentiments were being expressed throughout the room as to how much they all liked the new atmosphere. Some did convey it would be nice to have a dance floor. That would take some major dealings with the limited space available. Besides, it was a lounge not a club; that was the difference. There was a terrace with a beautiful garden and seating right outside the room. Maybe in the future, they could work something out and have a club on the premises. But right now her goal was to involve the entire community, and she had ideas for that, as well.

"Ms. Newton, you don't have to do that, I can for send Roy."

She glanced at his name tag since she preferred to address people by their name. "Stanley, I can straighten the table while you and Roy are in the back. Be sure to keep your count as accurate as possible on how many times you've made replacements of everything. That will help us with our inventory."

"Yes, Ma'am."

Ryane smiled. She hated to be referred to as Ms. or Ma'am, but she knew that was a sign of respect for her position in spite of her age...

Dang, the parking lot was packed. Chancey knew it was Friday night, but this was an unusual crowd for the hotel. What in the world was going on, he wondered, as he pulled up on the side of the lobby door? That was his private parking spot whenever he came to the hotel. He preferred being able to keep an eye on his black beauty himself. The valet attendant rushed to his door and opened it. He gave him a hundred dollar bill and walked off with his keys in his pocket like always.

"Good evening, Mr. McGowan."

He nodded hello and then asked what was going on and pointed to the parking lot across the street. The security guard told him new management and free food in the lounge.

"Whoa, sister ain't *playin,* is she?"

"No, Sir," said the security guard. "And Mr. McGowan, the way things are going, I don't think you'll be able to park your car there anymore. We're undergoing lots of new changes. "

He looked at the man he'd known all his life. "Mr. Wade, you let me handle the new management." He put a big grin on his handsome face and strolled off. Hell, he was the man. But once he had his dinner he ordered from the dining room, he'd have to check the lounge out. Chancey took out his cell and called the dining room. "This is Mr. McGowan, I'm in the hotel."

"Your dinner will be right out, sir." Chancey McGowan had his own designated spot where he liked to take his meals if not in the penthouse. A nice secluded area in the lobby window tucked away behind the large plant he purchased himself along with the beautiful fountain garden located in the middle of the lobby…

Ryane, still too excited to eat, visited the bar next. According to the bartender, no one had complained about prices of the non-alcoholic drinks which was music to her ears. She then thought she would walk out into the corridor and ran right into one of the room service attendants. Instead of going to the elevator he headed in the direction of the main lobby.

"Excuse me, but where are you going with that cart?"

The bellman nodded towards the main lobby instead of speaking.

"Stop right there," Ryane ordered sternly and with much attitude. "Now again I ask, where are you going with that cart?" She looked at his name plate. "Jeremy? Better yet, you take it back to the kitchen and wait for me."

Security came around the corner. Chancey was standing at the reception desk with the hotel clerk, watching.

"Ms. Newton, is there a problem?"

"Nothing I can't handle."

"Ms. Newton, ma'am I didn't mean to be," Jeremy

began to stutter..."BBBut this is for—"

"I don't care if it's for Chancey McGowan, himself. You will not push a food cart through my lobby. Now who is this for?" The expressions on the two men's faces said that was exactly who it was for, when a deep rich penetrating voice answered her. She snatched around to face the man and knew he was beyond being good-looking. He would certainly make the top ten's list for most handsome. Ryane boldly took a quick study of the fine specimen standing and smiling before her. Smooth, chocolate complexion with a swirl of cream; tall with wide, powerful shoulders; thick, firm chest; mesmerizing smile; dark, thick, smooth lips, with a medium neatly-trimmed mustache that was connected to a light beard. What Shelly said came to mind, and she didn't exaggerate one bit about the sophisticated, sexy player. All the man said was **ME** and she was flushed. But that was impossible; she'd vowed to never become interested in another woman's son. She didn't care how handsome and fine he was, because she vowed never to become seriously involved ever again.

"Ms. Newton, where would you like for me to have my meal?" Being so close, he was engrossed with the total woman from head to toe as he waited for her response.

Oooo, she was having a hard time getting out what she had been prepared to say. "Mr. McGowan, you may have your dinner wherever you like tonight. But please, in the future, have your meals in the dining room or your penthouse." She knew he and his grandfather owned two thirds of Allanville Inn and he had a luxurious penthouse on the top floor.

"Yes, ma'am," he said with her walking off but not

before seeing a Porsche Cayenne in the lobby window.

She turned and looked back at him.

"I know, and I'll refrain from parking there as well," he stated with a fetching grin, undressing her with his dreamy, penetrating eyes.

"Thank you, Mr. McGowan," replied Ryane, walking off with his gaze following, watching the sway of her ample hips. He vowed to get his appetite good and whet with some Ms. Newton real soon, at whatever cost.

"Jeremy, I'm sure my dinner is cold; take care of it for me and have Chef to put a little extra along with another place setting and bring it to the lounge. I'm sure Ms. Newton won't mind since they are serving food there. And Wade, will you have my Cayenne moved?"

They both said, "Yes, sir."

Chancey winked at the three men and strolled to the lounge...

"Where have you been, better yet, what have you been doing? You're perspiring." Shelly gave her a napkin and signaled for a waitress so she could order her something nice and cold.

Ryane leaned over to whisper that she'd met the incoercible Chancey McGowan when she sensed his presence along with every female in the room. Once again, Shelly didn't exaggerate.

Vic stood. "Chancey, it's good to see you, man."

Chancey spoke but not once did he take his eyes

from her attractive face. Ryane was breathtaking, especially when she was flushed. She was certainly high-maintenance, which was understandable in her profession. Manicured nails and toes, stylish, beauty salon hair and arched eyebrows, dreamy, dark-brown eyes he noticed lit up when she was excited, kissable, inviting lips, and smooth, velvety skin that entreated caressing; that was Ms. Ryane Newton. *Patience, Rocky, I do understand.*

"You remember Shelly? And this is our new hotel executive."

"Shelly, you get prettier every time I see you," he said, winking and giving her an appreciative smile. Then he turned his gaze back to Ryane. "I've had the pleasure of meeting Ms. Newton in the course of some unnecessary circumstances that I hope we can put behind us. And I would like to offer my sincerest apology, Ms. Newton."

Oooo, his smile was spellbinding and his piercing gaze was like a magnetic force, drawing her in. She blinked to break his hold with three pairs of eyes glancing at her and then him. "Of course, Mr. McGowan, apology accepted."

"Thank you and please call me, Chancey. That's what my friends call me and I hope you and I will become friends." He held his hand out and she accepted, which was a major mistake. His caressing handshake was unnerving every cell in her body, while igniting them into individual sparks. She needed something cold, and in a hurry, to put out the blazing fire that began to consume her insides. OMG, from just a handshake, she thought. She and Justin would kiss and she'd never felt what she was feeling at that very moment. What was it about this man?

"Say man, why don't you keep the ladies company, I need to get home," announced Vic. "You know we're expecting our second baby and I promised my wife not to stay long. So, ladies, I'm going to say good night and I'll see you tomorrow, Chancey."

While they did that brother handshake ritual, Shelly dropped a bomb and said she needed to leave, as well. She gave some flimsy excuse about having to drive their grandmother and aunts to Bellville for a Ladies' Day Program in the morning. That was the first time she mentioned that and Ryane was sure they'd bailed out on her because of him as she watched them disappeared into the crowd.

CHAPTER EIGHT

Chancey smiled as he signaled to the waiter who was bringing his dinner. It couldn't have worked out any better if he had planned it himself, he thought as he sat beside her.

"So Mr., I mean, Chancey, what made you change your mind about eating in the lobby?"

"You might say the scenery is much lovelier here than out there," he said, wooing her with his sensuous voice and penetrating, playful gaze.

"Mr. McGowan, your dinner sir," said the bellman.

Mmmm, whatever he ordered smelled delicious. Her grumbling stomach was a reminder that she hadn't eaten since her early lunch. Ryane watched the bellman uncover his platter and was certain she drooled and gently patted her mouth.

"Thanks Jeremy," said Chancey. "I can take it from here." He set the extra place setting in front of her. "Ryane being the busy and conscientious executive I know you are, you've probably neglected to have dinner. I insist you share mine." He then began to serve her a portion of his roasted, diced potatoes, broccoli, salmon croquettes, and dinner salad.

She looked at him in awe as he filled her plate. What did he know about her work ethics or was it a lucky guess? Regardless, he was right and she was starving.

"Thanks, Chancey, I could eat a—" She stopped with what she was going to say.

He flashed his sexy smile and said, "Me too," and leaned over to put dressing on her salad.

The man just oozed sex appeal by the gallon, and smelled divine. Ryane didn't recognize the name of his manly scent, an expensive one no doubt since everything about him screamed money. Inhaling his fragrance was like a drug taking control of her mind, causing her to think of all kinds of intimate acts she wanted to occur with him only. Again, Shelly didn't exaggerate one bit. She was behaving like all the other women. Wicked thoughts plagued her mind; that was what this man caused her to have. Justin certainly didn't and she loved him. Was that possible? Tainted lust was the only explanation for what she was experiencing. As he blessed their meal, she silently asked for forgiveness. They began to eat in a peaceful quietness, enjoying the soothing music in spite of them being in a room full of people. Both stole glances at one another from time to time thinking neither was aware.

"Would you like some more?" he asked.

"No, I've had enough, thank you," said Ryane, ignoring the fact that he had been watching her sop up the rest of her sauce with a roll, and she could care less. She was being herself.

"How about dessert? They serve the best key lime pie, ever."

"Sure, that sounds great."

He signaled for a waitress; two rushed to his side.

One was asked to clear the table and the other to get the dessert. Both were tipped well Ryane was sure.

"So, Ryane, tell me about Ms. Newton besides her being a beautiful and desirable woman." He leaned back in his chair and again awarded her his fetching smile.

She had his undivided attention for whatever she was willing to share. Ryane concluded that Chancey McGowan was smooth with words to match his good looks, down to his unquestionably player character. As far as she was concerned there was nothing to tell, or at least nothing she wanted to say to him. Then again, maybe she would allow him into her world. Hopefully, he'd then get the message she was not looking for a man at the present time in spite of him having cast a spell on her with her insides quivering down to her female core.

"Well, Chancey in a few words, I'm an angry black woman with a serious attitude who's not looking for a monogamous relationship for the next fifty years. I've done that."

"So, you're saying no love or commitments, just participate in a little grown folks fun with *no strings attached.*"

"You hit it on the nail," she said and took a sip of her drink. "And I may add, that's when I have the urge to do so." She put extra emphasis on the word *I* and pointed to herself.

"May I ask what caused you to feel this way?" he asked, like he didn't already know. He just wanted to see if she was going to say why.

"My sister and fiancé, who's now my brother-in-law, slept together and now they're expecting their first baby." She spoke the words bluntly without any feelings one way or the other and was sure she shocked him as well.

"Don't you think that's taking drastic measures behind one failed relationship, and fifty years? Ryane you'll be—"

She interrupted him, "Eighty-two."

"What about children? Surely you want to be a mother and soon."

Ryane knew exactly what he meant; she was already thirty-two. "Yes, I do and plan to have at least two by the same man."

He looked at her with a raised brow. Ryane Newton had given this some serious thought.

"And I don't have to be married to do so. I'm sure you know that," She stated clearly in a cantankerous voice. But he continued with his inquest anyway.

"What about the father of your children?"

"What about him?"

"What if he wants to be a part of his children's lives?"

"He can as long as he understands he should concern himself with his children, and not their mother, me."

The daughter of an elder talking like that had Chancey wondering, was she through with the church as well, since her fiancé was a minister.

"What will your parents say?"

"Nothing, I am a grown woman and they'll have to accept my decision. All I need is someone who will accept and understand my wishes and philosophy. So enough about me, why aren't you married and do you ever plan to have children?" She emphasized the word children. "And please don't insult my intelligence and say you haven't found the right one yet. Good women are a dime a dozen. It's men like you that cause us pain and hurt when you reject our love and treat us unfairly."

"Whoa, Ryane, slow down, I'm not guilty of doing any of that and yes, I would love to have children in the future, once I do find the right woman."

"Really, Chancey, you're the kind of man that attracts women like flies and yet none of them have been good enough for you to marry or give you a baby? You could have saved that remark."

He wanted to know right off the top where her head was since she'd been studying him, no doubt sizing him up. "Are you considering me as a prospect," he asked and took a big swallow of his drink.

She gave him a serious look and simply replied, "Maybe."

He strangled and began a series of coughs.

"Are you all right?" she asked and hit him a couple of times in the back. She figured it was what she said that caught him off guard.

He held his hand up for her to stop and took another sip. Chancey whispered, "I'm good, you can stop with the beating."

"Fine, and for the record, please don't get all bent out of shape if I decide you're the one. Trust me, you will not be obligated for anything except pure satisfaction, and that's a promise." He was right about one thing; she was not getting any younger and may as well consider the possibility of becoming a mother.

The waitress arrived with their dessert, which put an end to the conversation. He was glad of that because Ryane Newton had just propositioned him in a subtle manner and that needed to be discussed in private. He thanked the waitress and took the dessert plate out of her hand and set it on the table between them. Ryane gave him a puzzled look. "Trust me, it's more than enough," he said because he no longer had a taste for pie unless he was licking it off of her, especially after her revelation.

Ryane was about to say speak for yourself because she needed her fix. When he uncovered the pie and she saw it was a piece big enough for two greedy people, she decided to keep her comment.

Picking up the spoon, he said, "Please, allow me."

She did.

He fed her a spoonful of the pie and waited for her response.

"Mmmm," she moaned with her eyes closed. The rich, creamy filling was mouthwatering.

"Pleased?"

72

"Oh, yes."

And so was he in more ways than one. Chancey McGowan had the hots for Ryane Newton and she was not going to make it difficult for them to have some serious sex. He just needed to be sure he was ready to be with a woman like her. She would not be easy to walk away from, even with her claiming she wasn't looking for a relationship. That wouldn't last long at all. She had been raised to fall in love, have a family, and live a good life. Anyway, fatherhood was not an option right now. His kind of business was not suitable for a family. He gave her another spoonful and her reaction was the same. If it had been anyone else, he would have taken her response as an act of pure seduction after what she'd just revealed. But babygirl was merely enjoying the pie, he decided as he watched her savor each drop. He just wished his body believed so!

"Girl, if you don't stop that you're going to get more than pie."

"What?" she asked innocently.

He imitated her sensual moans with much exaggeration.

"I did not sound like that," she said in defense. "You know you're overdoing it."

"Oh yeah." He tried to give her another spoonful, but she pressed her lips tightly together. Pie filling was all over her lips.

"Look what you did," she said excitedly, trying to lick it off.

"Let me," slipped out of his mouth before he knew it. He then began kissing away the sweet filling, not caring that they were in a public place, his hotel, and with his executive manager. No denying, she was incredibly sexy and had just made it clear, she was looking for sex and somebody to be her baby's daddy.

Ryane knew she should have stopped him, but why? She was enjoying every bit of it. Justin never kissed her mouth clean. Mr. McGowan got an *A* for cleaning up behind himself, even if it was an act of seduction.

"Is it all gone?" she asked sticking out her satiny tongue.

He watched it dart in and out and wondered how it tasted. "Ryane, don't do that," he pleaded.

She smiled. That'll teach him to mock her, she thought and licked her lips once again.

He signaled for a waitress. "Come on, we're leaving."

"What about my pie?"

"I'll get you a carry out." Tasting her lips was too much and he had to get up outta there ASAP. She was causing him to lose his cool and no woman has ever done that. He'd always had control of the situation. But it had been a minute since he'd had some grown and sexy fun.

"I can't leave, Mr. McGowan. The lounge will be open for another two hours."

"Don't you start that 'Mr. McGowan' nonsense. And who says you have to stay until closing time? You're in

74

charge, remember." The waitress was back. He gave Ryane her black satin pouch and held her chair.

She could tell he was quite serious. To keep from making another scene with him, she got up. He took her hand and led her out.

Once they were outside, Ryane stopped. "Now where are we going, Chancey?"

"To the penthouse for privacy and to continue our conversation," he said, leading her to the elevator.

"No, not the penthouse," she said forcefully, looking at her watch. "I've had a long day and I'm tired."

Disappointment was an understatement. He wasn't ready for them to call it an evening even if he did understand. Chancey admitted to himself that he loved being with her. Furthermore, he wanted to discuss what she had put on his mind. But first he needed to ask himself whether or not he was in fact ready to begin a family.

"Ryane, you're breaking my heart and killing me all at the same time," he said with his hand over it.

"Believe me, you'll survive," she said sarcastically. "You know the old saying: what doesn't kill us makes us stronger. I'm a living example."

"No, Ryane, you were already a strong person. What's happened has turned you into an angry black woman." The hurt that shadowed her face crushed him and he knew what he said only added salt to her wound. It was all right for her to refer to herself as such but not him.

She didn't respond, instead she said good night, walking off with her eyes filling up with tears.

He started to run after her but decided to leave well enough alone. Tomorrow was another day and she would certainly need company.

CHAPTER NINE

Ryane had been up for hours, had taken a bath and was fully dressed in a yellow-print, strapless dress and matching sandals since she couldn't sleep. She even played in her hair for a while, trying different styles. At dawn, she watched the glorious sunrise and was thankful she was alive in spite of feeling empty inside. Today was supposed to have been her special day, but thanks to two people she loved dearly, it was ruined.

The church was to be decorated in vivid shades of coral, beautiful bows, lovely flowers with lush greenery, a plant stand arch, and yards of chiffon draped throughout the sanctuary. So much for what should have happened, thought Ryane as she brushed a tear from her face. She stepped out on her front porch and chose to sit a spell and enjoy Allanville's splendid spring morning before going to the hotel. She decided that until she was familiar with the employees, she wanted to make her presence known. Yes, she was using the hotel as an excuse to occupy her time and why not? There was nothing else for her to do today. She needed to stay busy.

Shelly texted to see what happened when she left, but Ryane refused to elaborate until they saw each other later. But she did have a word or two to tell her for abandoning her with that Chancey McGowan. How dare he accuse her of being angry? Did he hear what she said about her sister and fiancé? Nonetheless, she let him know who he was tangling with. Her cell rang.

"Hi, Mother…yes, I've been up for hours…I haven't planned anything for today. I'm going to the hotel for a little while and then stop at the deli…How are the folks? Tell my grandparents I miss them terribly…Mother, Easter is just too soon…Somebody else can do the egg hunt. To be honest, Mother, let Rena take over all of my activities since she wanted my man."

"Ryane, please let go of the anger. It's not healthy, baby."

"Mother, I can't help it. My life has been turned upside down because of them, so please understand if I choose to hang onto my ill feelings at least for a little while."

"Baby, I know you've been hurt and today was supposed to be your wedding day; I'm pleading with you to not allow all this hostility to consume you much longer. Now, let's change the subject, if Easter is too soon, what about Mother's Day?"

She hated to disappoint her mother and grandmothers on this day. The males of both families have always made that day very special. But with Rena expecting her first child by way of her ex-fiancé, she did not think she could handle that right now. "Mother, I just can't promise you I'll be home for Mother's Day. In all honesty, the way I feel, I don't know when I'll return to Texarkana." She was beginning to get emotional and didn't want to cry. "I know this will be the first time and I hate to disappoint you Mother, but give me until the end of April before I make a decision to come or not. And I promise to work on my disposition." She sniffed back a cry. "Someone is at my front door; I'll call you tomorrow after I think you're home from dinner…Yes, Mother, I'm going to their 7:15 service. Don't worry, I'll never leave the church...Love you too Mother, and give my love to Daddy...Bye."

Ryane set her cell down and went to see who was making an early morning call. She couldn't imagine who was paying her a visit. The Anderson women were in Bellville for their annual Ladies' Day program. She peeped out her front window before opening her door and couldn't believe Chancey McGowan had invited himself to her home. She was in a bad mood and not up to this, she thought, opening her door.

"Good morning, sunshine!"

Was he trying to be funny? Her disposition hadn't changed. It was still the same as last night when they parted. Dang, this man was fine and looked like a top fashion model whose job was to sell designer jeans. The bright red polo t-shirt that was open at the neck and stretched across his broad chest had his chocolate swirl complexion glowing.

"Morning, and how may I help you?" she said dryly.

"I see our mood has not changed. Maybe this will help some." He handed her a masterpiece floral arrangement in vivid colors of rose, yellow, and blue: daffodils, daisies, and pansies.

Her mouth formed the perfect **O**. "Chancey, they're absolutely gorgeous, thank you. Please come in."

That's better, he thought as he followed her.

"I need to find the perfect place for these," she said, looking around her small living area.

79

"How about there?" he said, pointing to a three shelf accent table that was in her front window. "You can move your candles to the bottom shelf."

She surprised him by following his suggestion. She bent over, showing the shape of her luscious behind.

"Now they can be seen from the street. Thanks again, Chancey, that was so thoughtful and sweet of you. You can't imagine how much you've lifted my spirits."

For the first time, he saw warmth and tenderness instead of anger and bitterness. Naturally, he was aware of what today was, and knew she needed some TLC.

"What's in the bag?"

"Ingredients for breakfast and a little extra," he replied.

"Ingredients, who's cooking?" she asked.

"Me," he exclaimed. Chancey went straight to her kitchen and began to get familiar with where she stored things. He opened drawers and cabinets to find everything needed.

"What are you going to make?"

"Cheese omelets with sausage and bacon, croissants, fresh fruit, and juice," he said. "Come and keep me company."

Wow, she thought, and joined him in the kitchen. "What can I do to help?"

"Just continue to look like beautiful sunshine and keep me company. Oh, and make some dishwater. I like to clean as I cook."

She did and made a mental note of the qualities he'd demonstrated so far. They also engaged in simple conversation, nothing as heavy as last night. He wanted to know about her plans for today as he moved around preparing their meal. It was evident he knew his way around a kitchen. Ryane told him she wanted to visit the hotel for an hour or so and then return home. After passing time talking about nothing in general, the stove's timer went off; the croissants were done and the fruit was cut up.

"Ryane, you can start setting up. Fill our glasses with the juice I put in your fridge and put the condiments on the table," instructed Chancey while he began to fill the platter. He gave it a restaurant flavor with fresh parsley he found in her fridge when he put in the juice.

She looked at him with a strange expression.

"What is it?" Everything looked attractive and appetizing.

"How about we dine in the living room, then I can look at my flowers while we eat. I can set up a folding table and put a tablecloth on it."

"That's fine, Ryane," he said to her back.

She was already pulling a table out of her closet along with a lemon yellow, jacquard-print tablecloth. She removed the two place settings from her table and put them down.

"I'll be right back," she announced as she rushed out her back door with the flirty tail of her short dress flying behind her. A few minutes later, she returned with a couple of blooms from her own flower bed and arranged them in a vase while he set the food on the table. "Now we're surrounded by sunshine," said Ryane with a smile of approval.

They took a seat, said grace, and began to eat.

"Mmmmm, delicious," she moaned.

"Ryane, please don't start that again."

She gave him a **REALLY** gaze and continued to enjoy her meal but tried to be mindful of his plea to refrain from the moans.

"Mr. McGowan, you do have skills."

"Thanks, Ms. Newton, wait until you taste my barbecue."

"Mmmm, I can't wait," she moaned and gave him a wink. They continued their meal, engaging in light conversation…

"No, you don't," said Ryane, pushing Chancey past the sofa to the front door. "We're going for a walk after eating all those calories."

"I don't feel like exercising. You know men like to sit and let their food digest. Besides, I did three laps this morning."

"Let's compromise and walk to the end of the corner and back."

He agreed and they left for their short stroll; at least that's what she led him to think. Once they got to the end of the corner, she was going to insist they make the block.

"Don't think I'm going to give in to your every whim, Ms. Newton," he said, giving her hand a gentle squeeze as they strolled down her street.

"Will you stop and enjoy this beautiful day God has given us?" Ryane expressed.

He detected she was becoming a little testy and decided the less said was best. A nice quiet walk was what she needed.

Ryane knew she was being temperamental but she couldn't help it. She was sure Chancey McGowan had a hidden agenda to put another notch on his bed post; after all, he was Allanville's stud. No, he did not do the local sisters, just those new to the area. But this time, the shoe was put on the other foot, and he had something to think about when he hit on her. She had been so sure that after last night he would have made himself scarce. Instead, he showed up on her doorstep with flowers and food. One thing was for sure: she knew what he was about, his intentions, and could care less one way or the other.

Her neighborhood was a peaceful and quiet little haven, thought Ryane as they turned the corner. He never mumbled a word, just held her hand and followed. Most of the yards were free of children today. She guessed this was a day of relaxation for grandparents. "Wow, something big is going on somewhere on this street; look at all the cars. They're everywhere," she exclaimed, pointing.

Dang, he forgot the Johnson's oldest daughter, Maureen, was having a backyard wedding today. He needed to get her off this street in a hurry without upsetting her. "Okay, we walked to the corner and halfway, I'm ready to turn around."

"Oooo, you're such a ninny. Like you said, we're halfway, let's just make the block since that will put us right at my house once we turn the corner." They continued with her practically pulling him along when she recognized Shelly. She was surprised to see they were back from the program already. Ryane waited for her to finish parking her car so she could speak and be nosey at the same time.

"Hey, Shelly," the couple said together

"Hey, Ryane...Chancey, I thought I recognized you two when I passed the first time from dropping *Dear-Dear* and Auntie off." She studied them closely. "So, what have you two been up to?" Shelly asked with a smile that said, *I caught cha*.

Ryane picked up on what she didn't say but was very much implied.

"We had a delicious, late breakfast and Ryane insisted we take a walk. I, on the other hand, wanted to just lie around," said Chancey, feeding into what she wanted to hear.

Ryane caught that, too. "You two need to quit with all the insinuations. He invited himself to my home and prepared a big breakfast. It was no way we were going to lie around. Now what's happening on this street?" asked Ryane.

Before Shelly could answer her question, Chancey continued with his teasing. "You know your friend here is unappreciative. I slaved over a hot stove to fix her a nutritious breakfast and this is the thanks I get."

Ryane looked with that *I don't believe you* expression and said, "Shelly, please ignore him. He's whined practically the entire walk. Next time, I'll just leave him at the house."

"Oh, there's going to be a next time?" asked Shelly. He hadn't taken his eyes off of her the whole time, which was answer enough for her.

"Shelly, will you please stop and tell me what's going on?"

"Maureen Johnson is having a wedding in her parents' backyard."

"A wedding," said Ryane and repeated the words again.

Me and my big mouth, thought Shelly as she watched Ryane's face become colored in sadness while tears filled her eyes.

Without a word spoken, Ryane walked away. They both called out with her increasing her pace.

"Go ahead to the wedding, Shelly. I'll take care of her," yelled Chancey, jogging off to catch her. *That was the purpose of him trying to turn her around when he first saw the street full of cars.*

Shelly felt terrible for speaking the **w** word. Ryane seemed to have given her idea of not getting involved again some serious thought and she was thankful Chancey McGowan was able to arouse her interest. If anyone could change her mind, it was him with all his charm and finesse. But she'd have Vic put a bug in his grandfather's ear, because she refused to stand by and let him cause her more pain.

Chancey caught up with her and tried to hold her hand; she snatched away. He knew talking about it was not the answer for now. They walked in silence with her wiping fallen tears. When they turned the corner, she started running and was on her front porch in seconds. She struggled with the unlocked door but finally got it open and tried to slam it closed. He guessed she thought that would keep him out. But she didn't need to be alone, nor would she. He put his hand out to keep the door from closing, which wasn't a smart thing. But the pain he experienced for doing so was worth it as he stepped across her threshold. She was on her knees rocking and crying loud, heart-aching sobs that pulled at the core of his soul. He knelt beside her to console her. She pushed him away and continued to weep and rock. After a few seconds of watching and listening to her carry on in such a pitiful way, he pulled her into his powerful arms despite her protest.

"No...no...no," she screamed over and over through her sobs. When he didn't let go, she attempted to hit him but he pinned her arms and legs down with his strong limbs and continued to hold and rock her in a soothing manner. For a few minutes, she forgot where she was and who she was with as she screamed her head off for Justin to let go of her. Bucking like a wild, unbroken stallion, she tried breaking out of his steel-trap hold but it was useless. Hearing her scream his name, Chancey knew then that was why she was behaving so violently, she thought he was Justin.

"Ryane, sweetheart, open your eyes. Open your eyes, baby," he coaxed. "I'm not Justin. I'm not Justin," he repeated several times. "He's not here."

After a few seconds she did as he requested and looked around. Pushing out intense breaths of air, she then realized he was not Justin, but Chancey...Chancey McGowan. He released his tight grip which allowed her to pull away. She turned over in a fetal position and gently rocked her aching body. "Oh God, it's not fair." She began stammering and ranting, "today should have been my wedding day...walking down the aisle with my daddy...in my beautiful dress...veil...bridal bouquet...it's not fair... it's just not fair." Her heartbreaking sobs began all over again.

Chancey pulled her back into his arms and held her tightly to his chiseled chest. He planted soothing kisses on her face as he rocked her gently. After her crying slowed down to a whimper, Ryane allowed him to assist her to stand. With her wet face buried in his chest he walked her lifeless body to her bedroom.

She gathered every ounce of strength to move her feet which felt like tons of bricks. Once they got to her bed, she willed her struggling body to crawl upon the stack of pillows, exposing healthy thighs and luscious cheeks.

Chancey knew he should have been ashamed for the thoughts that ran through his mind as he watched the movement of her ample behind. Her delectable brown-sugar body caused sensational stirrings within his throbbing body that couldn't be ignored, Rocky made sure of that. His penetrating, dark eyes visualized her completely nude and stretched out on her queen-size bed, reaching for him. He wanted to crawl in beside her but knew that would not be wise or fair in her state of mind.

He removed her shoes and placed them on the floor. Looking around for something to cover her with, he spotted a light weight throw on her chaise to use. He kissed her tenderly on the cheek before he moved away from the bed.

"Please don't leave me," she sniveled. "I don't want to be alone."

"Okay, I'll be over here," said Chancey, pointing to her blue-figured chaise. He thought he would wait until she dropped off to sleep and then prepare a meal while she took a nap.

"No, I want you to hold me," she said, catching his hand.

Ryane was breaking his heart and had no idea the position she was putting him in or the pressure he was feeling. Okay, Chancey, you can do this, he said mentally and slipped out of his shoes and crawled in beside her. He put one arm around her waist and the other over her head to caress and move her damp hair out of her face. She began to gently rock which was a calming and comforting effect for her, but not for him. But he reassured himself he could do this as long as his manhood stayed intact! The million dollar question, how long could it with her rubbing against him, causing Rocky to react with each movement.

Ryane abruptly sat up and pitched her throw. "Help me out of this dang thing," she snapped through her sniffling. She shocked him by pulling down the top of her dress.

"Girl, what are you getting ready to do?"

"Take off this devilish thing," she cried and turned her back to him, "now unfasten it!"

He only hesitated for a second, which was too long for her.

"Surely you've done this a few times in your quest?"

She was right he has done this numerous times because he was a breast and thigh man.

What was he going to do with Ryane Newton, he thought as he unsnapped her cream, strapless lace bra? When he touched her skin, she gasped and arched her back through all her tears. He pretended he didn't notice her reaction which was ridiculous when his body showed telltale signs as he felt the silkiness of her velvety skin.

"Thank you," she said and got back in her favorite position without giving what she'd had him do another thought. He debated whether or not to pull her back in his arms. She made the decision for him and snuggled up to him and started her rocking motion again.

Several minutes later, the sniffling and rocking ceased. He figured she had finally drifted off to sleep.

"Chancey, why do men say they love you?" She kept her face turned and continued throwing questions without stopping to get an answer. "Ask you to marry them, go through the motions of pretending to make plans to spend their lives with you and then cheat? Have sex with another woman? Why do men do those things?"

"Ryane, baby, I can't speak for all men, but I will say there are some who have set goals from the very beginning to misuse, mistreat, and abuse. Those women who are desperately lonely with low self-esteem and feel they must have a man in spite of their character generally fall prey to their lies and deceit." He stroked her silky-smooth skin the entire time he talked which, had a calming effect on her. "Then the next thing you know, they're caught up in a disillusion. It's now impossible for them to see what's actually happening. Therefore, they allow themselves to become deeper and deeper involved. That's when things get out of hand. Believe it or not, there are some men who experience the same devastations. So really and truly, there are no real honest answers because relationships are developed under different circumstances."

"I bet there are more women than men," she said bitterly. "I promise to never give my heart to another man so it can be stomped on." With that revelation she began to rock again, this time she drifted off into a sound sleep which was understandable with all the crying and ranting.

Chancey would rest his eyes for a quick minute if it wasn't for her scent reminding his senses what an attractive, desirable woman she was. Turning her over on her back, a peaceful calmness had claimed her flawless, pretty face. Instead of snoring, she made a sweet lulling, humming sound. He watched the rising movement of her breasts as she slept, wishing he could bury his face between them to inhale and taste their sweetness. Chancey caressed her soft cheek lightly before he carefully slid himself off her bed.

CHAPTER TEN

Ryane awakened, a bit disoriented with a pounding headache. What was more disappointing, her bed was empty. Chancey McGowan was no longer there, which was probably for the best if she really thought about the seriousness of her vulnerability. This was supposed to be her wedding night. She had waited so long to give her precious gift to the man she loved and was sure loved her. Nonetheless, it was Mr. McGowan's lingering masculine scent that was still present and filling her nostrils. If she closed her eyes, not only could she smell him, but she could also felt his powerful arms and chiseled, comforting body. She was sure Chancey had made a lot of women happy with his TLC. The man was not only drop dead gorgeous, his skills were lethal. She could only imagine how much passionate loving he was capable of giving. "Get a grip, Ryane, and take a shower," she scolded aloud...

Ryane completed her shower and sprayed her body down in her mild, scented oil fragrance. Instead of her lacy negligée her Nanny had bought for her wedding night, she put on a girly, oversized t-shirt and boy shorts. She swiped a tear and dared another to fall as she picked up her cell to see if anyone had called or texted. While sliding her finger across the screen, she could hear her name being called. Her mouth dropped. She couldn't believe he was calling and for what? She told his spoiled *azz* wife, now it's time to tell him.

"Ryane," Justin shouted.

"Put her on speaker," whispered Rena.

He did.

"I can't believe it's really you," stated Justin.

"Yes, it's me and I want to know what the hell do you want? I thought I made myself clear to Rena that we don't have anything to say to each other." Her voice was elevated now.

"Ryane, we just wanted to hear your voice and know how you're doing, that's all, baby.

"Baby…baby, don't you dare call me that. And as far as how I'm doing, what the hell do you expect me to say? You two have caused me nothing but embarrassment and pain-stricken grief. Now I want you to hear me and hear me well. Do not and I mean, do not, dial my damn number ever again."

Chancey heard her screaming and got up from the sofa and rushed to her bedroom. She was sitting on her bed. He listened as her sister and brother-in-law tried to talk to her. Of course, they were not getting anywhere.

"Ryane, please," begged Rena. Ryane could tell her sister was crying but she no longer cared.

"Rena, I told you before and I'm going to say this for the last time, keep your damn tears for somebody who cares because I don't give a good—"

"Ryane, don't," said Chancey taking her phone. "Baby, let it go. Don't allow them to upset you."

"Hello…hello, who is this?" asked Justin.

"I'm a friend."

"No!" She screamed. "You don't have to explain who you are to them. Disconnect them now!"

He did and then sat beside her. "Ryane," he said softly, "you have to calm down and get a grip on all of this."

She looked at him and patted her chest. "Tonight was supposed to be my wedding night. Instead of me making passionate love to the man I thought loved me, he screwed my sister. Do you hear what I'm saying? He screwed my sister!" She wiped fallen tears. "If you want me to calm down and get a grip as you say, then make love to me," she screamed.

"Ryane, you don't mean that, you're just upset and angry right now."

"Upset, angry, I'm furious, no… *pissst*. I was deceived by my precious sister and fiancé." She repeated herself, "Chancey, I want you to make love to me tonight." She began to pull her t-shirt over her head, exposing her plump grapefruit-size breasts. Perfect.

Dang, his mouth began to drool. "Ryane…don't, baby." He caught her hands as she began to shimmy out of her boy shorts.

She wiggled out of them, her breasts jiggled with each movement. Her fleshy, nude body was perfectly proportioned and desirously beautiful and he couldn't wait to pleasure her completely. She had a small pouch of a stomach with an adorable navel that begged for his attention. She surprised him by having the cutest tattoo of

93

a dainty rose vine on her right breast extending to her cute, buttoned navel. An impressive work of art which was the first place he intended to taste.

She watched him scan her body and was not going to take a chance on him changing his mind. Although Ryane felt good about how she looked, she knew being overweight was a turnoff for some men. She had worked hard to have this body she now had and besides, she wanted this bad. "I want you to be my first with *no strings attached*. Please don't disappoint me," she whispered and pulled at the jogging pants that he had changed into. "I've had enough of that to last a life time."

Chancey saw the sadness in her eyes and knew she thought he didn't find her desirable. He would just have to show her. He removed her hands and then turned to leave. His condoms were in his backpack.

"Where are you going?"

"To get something we'll need."

"No condoms! I told you before, what happens will happen, and nothing will be required of you."

"Are you sure, baby, because once we start there's no turning back," he stated and began to take off his sleeveless t-shirt. Their eyes locked as he silently thought she could forget about her philosophy. Ryane Newton was the one who needed to be sure, especially if she conceived.

She whispered, "Yes," with her eyes glued to his magnificent, sculptured chest and muscles that bulged with each movement he made. Tattooed on his impeccable left

94

peck was a flying eagle. A cross was located underneath with the words *dedicated to my fallen brothers.* As he discarded his jogging pants and briefs, her gaze followed them to the floor as she admired his well-toned physic. She stopped and stared at his male organ like she had never seen one before, and she hadn't. Pictures and movies didn't count. Ryane Newton knew she was in for a treat, even if she did have to ask as she examined him closely, and had no shame doing so. Why would she at this point of her life, especially after what she'd been through?

"Say hello, Rocky," he said with a grin. Their eyes were now fixed on each other. He opened his arms for her, keeping in mind not to rush in spite of Rocky standing at attention and him being overly anxious. This was her first time, and he would pleasure her virgin body until she was physically ready to accept Rocky. More so, his goal was simple: make sure she would allow no other man to have this cherished possession, the *Newton jewels.*

Without any hesitation, Ryane took a deep breath and boldly walked into his embrace. *Lawd,* he was fine, she thought as they fit snugly against each other, her feeling his hardness and him feeling her softness. She felt every single detail, especially his manhood. Her heart raced as butterflies danced franticly in the pit of her stomach.

He began trailing kisses down the side of her neck to her shoulders, grazing them with his moist tongue while swaying, moving their bodies intimately to the rhythm of their heartbeats. She gasped at the feel of his growing manhood against her nakedness. Her hot breath singed his skin, causing the blood to rush wildly through his veins.

He lifted her chin to kiss and taste the sweetness of her tender lips. Gently parting them with his sleek tongue, he began caressing the walls of her mouth, darting in and out, playing a wicked game of tag with hers. Suckling. Licking. Stroking. Squeezing. Roaming hands and tantalizing lips were all over her virgin body. Blending sounds of throaty moans and sensuous humming put them both in a heated, fervid state. He finally released her so they both could catch their breaths, but not for long. Still in each other's grasp, he showered her with kisses under her neck trailing them down the center of her heavy breasts. When he captured one of the plump nipples, his suckling tempo slow then fast caused her to scream his name as her jewels quivered. He continued holding her tight with his mouth taking turns on each breast and felt great pleasure in hearing his name being hummed. Sucking, plucking, squeezing. He then caught her by surprise when he lifted her off her feet and walked to the bed. He laid her down with still a mouthful of breast, driving her crazy while climbing on top. As if she knew what was going to happen next, she threw her head back, spread her legs with one word escaping her lips, "Rocky."

"Not yet, baby," he whispered and began doing what he'd yearn to do the minute she undressed—trace kisses along her lovely rose vine. While doing so, he caressed and stroked her middle down to her inner thighs. Stopping at her precious jewels, lingering for a short time, still trying not to rush it, had her shifting and shuddering with his gentle expert attention. He clamped down on her mouth in a tongue-lashing kiss, causing her to lose it, her body responding excitedly to cravings she felt in places she didn't know existed. Twisting and screaming to the top of her voice, igniting raw sensuous passion, an earth-shattering orgasm began to break her down.

96

"Now, baby," he said more for his benefit than hers. Not giving her a chance to recover completely, he suckled her moist skin, stopping under her breast while placing himself between her thighs.

"Hurry, Chancey," she moaned and scooted quickly in position to receive him as if he had commanded her to do so. She held her breath, anticipating pain but receiving pure pleasure instead with him gently biting and sucking her neck.

Kissing her wrists and the palms of her hands, he then placed them over her head. Humming sounds came from deep within as he masterfully eased Rocky into her feminine softness. Mere entry caused her to spin out of control with another orgasm. Her spasmic tremors and the wonderful feeling of her hot, wet tightness had him fighting to keep control. Pumping, thrusting, grinding slow then fast, another orgasm began to unfold. She inhaled a sharp desperate breath of air and grabbed each shoulder as he continued his smooth, rhythmic moves. Her body mimicked each move until she was overtaken by a monstrous wave of pleasure and screamed his name.

He no longer could hold out as he felt his potent juices explode from his body. They both screamed each other's names in unison until their voices died down to a hoarse, throaty cry with him collapsing on top of her.

Ryane soon felt him growing again. He flipped her over on her stomach and OMG! He began all over with another incredible round of powerful thrusting, grinding, and stroking, ending in an overwhelming orgasm that left them both in a blissful state.

As their uneven breathing slowed to a normal pace

he rolled on his back and pulled her on top. He kissed her moist forehead and tightened his arms around her, both satisfied with the calm, peaceful silence. The only sounds were their heartbeats beating the same tune. She leaned up and caressed his chin and kissed his lips.

"I'm not too heavy?"

"No, ma'am." Was she kidding? He and Rocky loved the weight of her thick softness. And would love to go another round, but knew her tender state couldn't withstand it for now.

"You and Rocky were absolutely wonderful, and thank you both for making this night unforgettable." She kept the mind-blowing experience to herself. That would be her secret.

"We do aim to please." He gave her a light pat on her butt and pulled the sheet over them. Ryane stroked his chest and pulled on a pebbled nipple, taking it into her hot mouth. She could feel him gulping a mouthful of air while drawing in his stomach muscles, letting out a deep moan. Mmmm, Chancey McGowan has a fabulous body, thought Ryane as she continued to touch and explore. Hard rippled muscles welcomed her soft touch along with his maleness.

He allowed her to explore his body until Rocky began to ache. He took control, and once again, began another sensuous round of the age-old mating ritual.

CHAPTER ELEVEN

Chancey nudged the lips of the snoring sleeping beauty cuddled in his arms. Gently stroking her baby-soft cheek, he knew what he suspected all along about her was absolutely correct. Ryane Newton had one sensuous sexual appetite and had flattered him immensely. After their last round, she passed smooth out but not before she had him singing in perfect harmony with her. He was utterly satisfied. Both of their bodies possessed telltale signs…His cell rang.

*

Mmmmm… Chancey McGowan was a man with some impressive skills for sure, Ryane thought while applying make up to the passion marks that were visible. Although she had a printed scarf draped around the high neckline of her blue sheath, she wasn't taking any chances. Ryane picked up her blue clutch that matched her shoes and headed to the door. Her plans were to sit in the back like she did last Sunday and leave right after the sermon. After a night of fornicating with very little regrets and having a hard time not keeping it off her mind, she thought that would be best.

She had no idea when Mr. McGowan left her bed after wearing her completely out with another round initiated by her. And every inch of her body screamed she had been sexed by the best. A smile crossed her lips as she recalled his words after she caught her breath. She began suckling his pebbled nipples, stroking his defined chest, when he moaned, *"Get Rocky ready if you want another round."* Really, now how could she pass up such an opportunity as that? *Oooh,* now she understood why Shelly and women in general, drooled and lusted over him. They could only speculate, but she was like the others who were fortunate enough to become familiar with the man in the biblical sense. Mr. McGowan was not only a sensual sexy lover, he was gentle and compassionate. After their lovemaking, he gave her a gentle wash that was a turn-on by itself, but she was in no position to do anything but enjoy. Ryane caressed her stomach and hoped that she was now carrying his baby. Again, there was no shame in her game. She was going to have what she wanted on her terms.

*

"No, ma'am, don't even try slipping out of here and not say anything to me," said Shelly, stopping her from getting in her SUV.

Ryane smiled and said, "I'm not going to *kiss'n tell,"* but removed her scarf and shimmied her dress up to her thighs and added, "at least not in public."

Shelly covered her mouth in delightful shock.

"Now I want to go by the hotel for a few minutes to show my face and then go home to get buck naked." She giggled.

"I bet you do if the rest of your body looks like that," exclaimed Shelly. "I got a taste for an old fashion cheese burger basket. What you say I meet you at the house in about an hour with two, my treat."

"Sounds like a plan, girlfriend, and don't forget a chocolate shake."

"You've had enough chocolate for a while, but I won't," joked Shelly. Her grin was as big as Ryane's. The friends departed...

Ryane couldn't believe she had actually been hoping to see his black *Cayenne* parked at the hotel and was sadly disappointed. She even hung around the a little longer than she planned. To pass the time, she talked to her parents, both set of grandparents and her best friend, Jackie. Of course, her grandmothers brought up the holidays. She had to tell them it would be some time before she could bring herself to come back to Texarkana, and begged them to understand. She and Jackie, on the other hand, cried more than they talked, especially when she told her about her emotional breakdown and Chancey McGowan. The best friends hated that their lives had been altered. Jackie was glad to hear she had befriended Shelly Roberts. Ryane told her she couldn't wait for them to meet and expressed that Shelly's personality was a combination of theirs; that was why they'd hit it off so well. They promised to plan a trip soon, and Jackie told her to be sure to include Shelly.

Afterwards, Ryane decided to leave. She stopped at the desk to make sure he wasn't on the premises with her conscious giving her a mind lashing. As if that wasn't enough, the very words she spoke to him—he wouldn't be held responsible for anything extra—plagued her mind continuously. Nevertheless, Ryane knew she needed to treat last night as what it was, her *booty call*. She now needed to show some remorse and continue with her new attitude and life in Allanville. And that was not going to be as easy as she thought!

*

       Chancey McGowan, better known as Chocolate Swirl, was called in and had to return to Houston, ASAP. It seemed the dude his team had been watching had been seen on the strip. He was soliciting and had gotten fresh, new bodies for his exclusive club along with passing some bills. The Ramirez brothers, Jackol and Chico, had their own private tropical island off the shores of the Gulf of Mexico with a beautiful resort that offered adult entertainment in every form and fashion. Their clientele consisted of people from all over the world, and the resort had been in operation for a few years. Both brothers were bold and savvy. Jackol, who was the leader in their operation, was daring, cautious, and smart. Chico, on the other hand, was greedy, simple, and the reason for their downfall. He made it possible for them to track him and his brother down when he was caught right in Chancey's backyard. For the last two years, the special force team he was a member of had been able to put their people in place to gather information needed to charge the two brothers and their silent partners with prostitution to money laundering and everything in between. Now it was show time.

       Federal agents were in incognito, stationed around the island and were now waiting on the head man, Black Thunder. He wanted everyone in place the week after their so called, Mardi Gras, that's when the plan would come full circle. There would be no guests at the resort, because the brothers and their trustworthy, not-so-loyal employees would be regrouping and restocking after the big celebration. This was Chancey's first assignment of this

102

nature, and would certainly be his last. He wasn't cut out for this *macho chitilians* action and now had a reason to put this fictitious, savvy, stud character to rest... Ryane Deneen Newton. Babygirl was special. Chancey couldn't restrain the rise of his anatomy or the smile on his face as he thought of her and their steamy, hot sex. As his boys *Ice and Thunder* would say, he was *wupped* and had *wimped* completely out and wasn't shame to admit it, even to himself.

He hated to leave without surprising her with breakfast in bed. She deserved to be treated special and especially by him, but time wouldn't permit, he was on the run. Chocolate Swirl had received the call he had been waiting for. Nonetheless, as he backed out her driveway, he pulled up behind the Jenkins's delivery truck. Just his good luck, they were out making a special delivery. He ordered an exquisite, potted rose bush for her front porch and delicious chocolates to be delivered after twelve. That and the card should make his intentions crystal clear. Ryane Newton may as well get ready, because when he returned it would be for good, and she could forget about her uncannying philosophy.

*Chitilians...*he didn't want any other man to touch her. She belonged to him, along with her so-called angry black woman attitude. He was pretty sure she would never be with another after last night. There was nothing angry about her last night. She was passionately hot-blooded and wonderfully sensuous. He could still feel her sultry breath, petal-soft lips, and scorching hands that had his skin seared forever. Babygirl had caused a burning sensational pain that no other woman had ever caused. She was the only who could render the first aid he needed. And if she couldn't, he was willing to suffer until she was able to. They were meant for each other, and he would never allow her to carry out her ridiculous plan of being alone. Not without him, and certainly not with his baby growing inside her...

"Swirl, you ready to do this, man?" asked Black Thunder. "You seem a bit occupied. I need you alert, my brother. A lot of people are depending on us."

"Yeah, Thunder, I'm good."

You could hear the excitement in Thunder's voice as they were given the okay to land. He lived for this kind of *chitilians*. Swirl just prayed everything would go according to plan and all would get out alive. The Ramirez brothers did have a small army to protect their establishment. Hopefully, their people had disarmed them and had taken control of the highpoints. According to their undercover messenger, all was well and just waiting for the arrival of their commanding officer, Colonel Alton Beasley, alias Black Thunder.

CHAPTER TWELVE

Ryane, Shelly, and Jenkins Florist pulled up together at her home and exited their vehicles. The ladies looked at the truck and then each other. They walked up the steps to her porch to wait for the delivery. Both mouths popped wide open when they saw the most beautiful rose bush and a mixture of colorful blooms in a large, wooden wheel barrel being wheeled up the sidewalk.

"Good afternoon, ladies," greeted Steven, the delivery man, as he handed her a big, giftwrapped box and card. "Ms. Newton, where would you like for me to put your plant?"

Shelly knew she had been caught by surprise and asked him to find the best spot for it. While doing so, he explained if she wasn't pleased, she could wheel it wherever she liked. He also explained the wheel barrel was actually durable plastic and easy to maneuver due to the wheels. "All right, ladies that will do it. Ms. Newton, here's the instructions on how to take care of your potted rose garden. Enjoy, and ya'll have a nice day."

Ryane looked at the box and back to the rose bush, "I wonder who sent these? They are awesome!" Who came to mind she refused to say. And if her suspicions were right, she was giving them away. "I hope they're not from Rena and her husband, because if they are, you can have them Shelly." Her words were laced with bitterness.

"I'll be more than happy to take them off your

hands, but read the card first, Ryane, before jumping to conclusions," demanded Shelly, following her inside the house. *She prayed they weren't from her sister and ex. That would not only upset her, she'd fall back into a funk.* Ryane dropped the card on the table with her flowers from yesterday and told Shelly to get comfortable, she would be right back.

"Girl, this is a beautiful bouquet. Need I ask who sent them to you?"

"No, ma'am," she yelled out, "Mr. McGowan."

"The man has good taste."

"Now, that's better," announced Ryane. "This is the closest I can get to being butt naked." Her off-the-shoulder, pink-flowered, lightweight cotton dress was airy and comfortable. Instead of sleeves, it had ruffles.

"Is that a rose vine tattoo?"

"Yes, ma'am, now let's eat!"

"Not until you open the card, I can't stand the suspense. I do believe you're in for a big surprise."

"And let my cheeseburger basket get cold, I don't think so."

"Auh, Boss Lady, stop being contrary."

Ryane smacked her lips and picked the card up to open it. The most beautiful water-colored rose vine was on the front with the words, *I'm sorry please forgive me.*

"See Shelly, I knew it; now my food is not going to digest properly." She opened it to look inside at the handwriting, but didn't recognize the penmanship. It wasn't from them.

Ryane, I deeply regret having to leave you this morning, but duty called. I wanted so much to be there to see your eyes flutter open and kiss them closed again and prepare you a well-deserved breakfast. So for that, again I'm sorry. You won't hear from me for a while, but please believe you will be in my thoughts constantly until we are together again. I hope I can wrap up my business soon, but I can't make any promises. The rose bush is to remind you of how beautiful and delectable you are. And for every bite of chocolate, hopefully, you'll think of me and how we shared one passionate, sizzling night. Oh and forget about the no strings attached philosophy. We're now connected with a strong cord.

Chancey

A cord…Unconsciously she caressed her stomach. She'd heard there were some men who were able to tell when they'd gotten a woman pregnant. Her Nanny said Pawpaw knew each time she conceived. *Well, that's what you wanted, girl.*

Shelly looked at her friend while she took a bite of her burger. "Speechless huh?"

"You can say that again, and that's all I have to say."

"Humph, girl, with that red and blue body, you don't need to say anything else. But I do want to know what you're going to do about him. That was sweet and thoughtful. And I do believe he really likes you."

107

"Shelly, he was nothing but a *booty call* at my request. But I can say this much: he was not what I expected. And I think it's safe to conclude he's positively full of surprises in every aspect. Need I say more again?"

"No, ma'am," sang Shelly. "Unless you want to tell me about his lovemaking, girlfriend to girlfriend," she added.

"Passionate…Gentle…Skillful…Fantastic. Magnificent…Awesome…And mind blowing."

"Okay, I get the picture."

"No, you don't have the full picture," retorted Ryane and pretended to pull her dress up.

Shelly covered her face and hollered for her to stop. They burst into giggles and Ryane reached for her chocolates.

"Of course, I don't have anyone to compare him to."

"Girl, surely you wouldn't want anyone else after what you just said, especially since he answered your *booty call,* as you say."

Ryane shook her head "no" and sat the box between them. "Certainly not, nonetheless, he's already missing in action. And I can't even get seconds or thirds."

"Ryane, you sound like—"

She interrupted her, "A woman who has had the most sensuous night of sex in her life. And who's honest enough to admit to her new BF she does not want or desire another man's touch but his."

"Girl, you're serious, huh?" Shelly wasn't expecting an answer; the bold-faced expression on Ryane's face and no shame anywhere revealed it all.

"Yes, ma'am. So, I guess I'll just have to treasure the experience and move on. Besides, it looks like I'm not going to have a choice," she paused, "he's not here." Ryane leaned her head back on her sofa and closed her eyes as she continued. "And this is not the first time a man has walked away from me. But this time, it was according to my rules." She then took the top off of the candy box and glanced over at Shelly before she took another bite of chocolate. "Mmmm, Chancey, why didn't I let you use protection?"

Shelly's mouth flew wide open and not for a piece of the delicious square she had in her hand. "You didn't," she moaned, and bit into her chocolate treat. "Mmmm, is right, but girl, what if?"

"Don't say it," pleaded Ryane. "I thought that was what I wanted, already told him about having two children and living happily ever after without the daddy."

"What romance novels have you been reading?"

"None. It's just that Justin and I had intentions of starting our family immediately. But thanks to my baby sister, he's starting one with her and with my luck, I may be starting one alone. As my Grandma would say, I had the nerve to buy the carriage before I purchased the horses." She tasted another chocolate. "Mmmm," moaned Ryane. "Shelly, how do you lose two men in less than a month? Answer me that!"

"I can't," Shelly exclaimed as she held a square and

put the whole piece in her mouth." Through chews, she said, "I know one thing, we better stop with all this sinful chocolate."

"Sinful is right...Girl it's sinful how fine his body looks with no clothes on." Ryane paused. "Muscles, biceps, triceps, and abs that beg to be caressed, kissed, sucked, and stroked."

"Mmmm, you don't say."

She shook her head yes with Shelly giving her the eye. "Okay Shelly, I confess; I'm like all the rest, intrigued and mesmerized with the renowned Chancey McGowan.

"No Girlfriend, I do believe you have a little more than a satisfied body, you wearing his brand."

The friends were now relaxing on the sofa, watching a movie starring *Queen Latifah* and *Common.* Ryane had put the candy in the fridge and brought them something healthy to snack on. "Shelly, what does Chancey actually do for a living?"

Shelly looked over at her friend before answering, wondering where was this coming from. "According to Vic, he works in Houston at one of the top black-owned hotels as a bartender."

"Why would he work in a hotel there and have part ownership in the one here?"

"That's a million dollar question. But if I had to come up with an answer, I would think the fast living and excitement of the big city. He's also in the reserve and called periodically for special assignments at times, that's involved."

110

"You think that's the business he was speaking of and that's why he can't call?"

"Could be, depending on the nature of the assignment he has."

"What if I'm pregnant?"

"Have your baby and make him pay child support regardless of you not needing it. And summon him for *booty calls.*"

"Girl, I was just talking and letting off steam. I'm not going to allow him to complicate my life like that."

"Do you want to have his baby?"

"Yes, and that's all I'm going to do. I'll be like all the other single mothers who are capable of supporting a baby without the help of the father. But I'm not going to lie, I sure wish I had let him use a condom. And most of all, I pray I'm not pregnant."

*

"Shelly Roberts, I can't believe I let you talk me into doing this." Ryane got out of her vehicle and gave the attendant her keys.

"Girl, all we're doing is going to a jazz concert. While doing so, you can check out the place since you've never been to the Grandeur Inn. And believe me, it is something to see. Now hush, and let's go have some fun.

"Good evening, ladies, don't you two look beautiful." They smiled and thanked the doorman as he told them to have a nice time. The first thing that caught

111

Ryane's eye was the lovely waterfall garden between exquisite columns that was located in the center of the lobby. Not only was it a beautiful sight, it gave the hotel a sense of sophistication and elegance along with providing a wonderful background for picture taking sessions. Beautiful chandeliers, fine hardwood floors with eye-catching runners, faux walls instead of wallpaper, intriguing, priceless African American art, and charming but practical, comfortable furniture was the decor. As they took the side door to the outside corridor from the concert hall, a medium-size waterfall was in front of the building with stone benches. Their hotel was somewhat a replica on a smaller scale, which was accommodating for their small town and country flair. Seeing the hotel and attending the concert was supposed to be the real reason for coming to H-town according to her friend, but her instincts said there was more.

Shelly knew she was checking the place out and realized by now the Allanville Inn was virtually a carbon copy of the Grandeur Inn thanks to the input of Chancey. The designing of the hotel was his project unbeknownst to most people until they visited this hotel. What set them apart were the breathtaking gardens, duck ponds, and the country cottage feel at their inn.

"Where are we sitting, although we may not have much choice?" asked Ryane. The place was practically full.

"Pretty ladies, do you have reservations?" asked the host.

Shelly told him they were in her name and he escorted them right to the spot she requested, near the bar. Shelly knew if Chancey McGowan was in town, he would be there for the jazz concert for sure.

"Ladies, please follow me."

Perfect, thought Shelly as they took their seats. They had an excellent view of the stage and close enough to the bar without being disturbed with the activity.

"Okay, Shelly, this was so sweet of you, but to go to this much trouble, really has it shown that much?"

"Yes, and it has been weeks. I hate I didn't follow you home that day and send him running."

"Listen and hear me well, I have no regrets and I'm good. We'll just say I did what was supposed to have been done on my wedding night. He was my personal wedding gift. And girlfriend, I have to say he was remarkable. It's just that I may have a receipt."

"That's another reason why I feel bad, Ryane. You won't take a pregnancy test or make an appointment, knowing prenatal care is—" Shelly stopped midway her sentence.

"Can I get you ladies something from the bar? We also have a delicious buffet," said the waitress. They ordered two nonalcoholic drinks and a sample platter.

Now that's service, thought Ryane, and a way to keep down unnecessary waste, at least to a limit. "As I was saying, it's been almost five weeks."

"I know, Shelly. I guess I just don't want to know yet. Give me until after Mother's Day. I promise to take the test then, and we can find out together if I am or not. Now let's not talk about it anymore and enjoy the concert, it's about to start."

And they did. Ryane was impressed with the trio's unique sound. Shelly said they were a local group, but the hotel also hosted performances by popular artists.

"Mmmm, this stuffed shrimp is delicious," whispered Ryane.

"Shush… listen."

"Isn't this a Chocolate Swirl production, where is Swirl?"

"Sweet Thang, Swirl has been AWOL for over a month. That fine Diamond came through and the rest is history. Nobody has seen or heard from him. You know he got it like that with management and disappears whenever Diamond shows up. Can I be of any service?"

"You're fine enough, but not tonight."

"Oh, you're breaking my heart," said the handsome honey-colored dude. "So Chocolate Swirl is the only flavor you have a taste for tonight?"

"You said it," replied the attractive, tall sister who switched off with much attitude.

"Man, you oughta quit. Once a woman has a taste of that Chocolate Swirl they're done." The two men bumped fists and chuckled as they left the bar.

A minute or two went by before either lady spoke with Ryane being the first. "Well, I guess I would be foolish to ponder over his whereabouts any longer and I won't. Thanks, Shelly, and I mean that from the bottom of my heart."

114

CHAPTER THIRTEEN

Ryane turned her lights off and secured her door before retreating to her bedroom. Her overnight bag was packed and placed in the chair for her early morning flight. Yep, she'd made the decision to go home for Mother's Day but would return on the same day. When she talked to her mother and grandmothers and told them she'd decided not to come, they'd become very emotional with her grandmothers expressing this could be their last Mother's Day. She tried to explain how she felt about seeing Rena and her cute baby bump as her Nanny called it. She even went as far as to say she would only put a damper on the holiday for everyone because she still had a foul attitude. That wasn't good enough for them. Yes, she'd forgiven but that did not say she did not want to whip Rena's *azz*, baby bump and all. After going back and forth with them saying she was the only gift they wanted, she still told them no. Secretly, she conceded with only Jackie knowing of her plans since she was picking her up from the airport. Text: *confirming pick up @ 7:30…can't wait 2 c u…Jackie*

Ryane was exhausted and hoped it wouldn't take her long to fall asleep. Although she'd spent long, late hours at the hotel for the last few weeks, her sleep still took its time coming. The hotel was doing extremely well. In addition to local and community affairs, they had three last-minute small group conferences back to back which had put them in the league with the bigger hotels. The buzz was that Allanville was a safe haven away from the big city's hustle and bustle along with providing excellent

115

service, accommodations, and good old southern hospitality. All were pleased and gave the hotel five-star reviews. They insisted on locking in their dates for the next year, making reservations in advance.

A new website and brochures had been designed, which has also boosted their business. She'd also had to hire an office manager to assist her. Ryane realized she couldn't make personal appearances in the community and manage her office at the same time, especially with the popularity of the lounge. She'd hired additional workers to serve patrons in the lounge for the buffet and other functions the hotel may have. That was a wonderful idea she picked up from the Grandeur Inn. She was still working on live entertainment, but that would have to come much later. The room was just not big enough. But the satellite music was working out great for the time being, and it was very economical. Needless to say, the shareholders were happy with her accomplishments in the short time she'd been there, all except one, Chancey McGowan. He was still missing in action.

It was like he had disappeared from the face of the earth. Even Vic said his grandfather and parents hadn't heard a word from him, but that was not unusual. According to Vic, it was his typical behavior. What she and Shelly overheard the night they went to the concert they'd kept to themselves, especially since no one had asked. The rose bush was gorgeous, and she and her staff enjoyed the remainder of the chocolates. Although she thought about him and their night of passion often, she was still taking each day at a time. What else could she do?

*

"Ryane, look at you," shouted Jackie as she stood with the other people who were picking up family members. The best friends embraced. "I can't believe you cut your long, gorgeous hair, but girlfriend, you look absolutely stunning. And that suit is fabulous."

She was dressed to impress in a beautiful, dark coral suit. The figure flattering jacket with a sculptured fabric rose and side gathers topped her long wrap skirt which exposed healthy thighs as she walked. Fancy gold jewelry, matching shoes, and a clutch accessorized her outfit. She even had a new haircut, a curly top with tapered sides and back.

"Thanks, Jackie, you look great yourself. What is that on your finger?"

She wiggled her ring finger. "Todd and I are engaged." She did tell her she had a surprise.

"That's wonderful. I'm so happy for you both." Todd and Justin had become best friends because of their relationships but Jackie said at the moment they were a little distant with all that had happened.

"Ryane, I declare, you look like a movie star, especially with those designer shades."

"Jackie, you need to quit," she said, actually blushing. She did turn several heads that morning. The bellman flat-out refused to accept her tip and wanted her phone number instead even when she told him he was too young and insisted he accept her bill.

"Well, I'm just telling you how I see you. Girl, you're wearing the title DIVA now."

"Thanks, friend."

"You're welcome, now are you ready for this?"

"About as ready as I'm going to be," she said and climbed into Jackie's BMW. Keeping what she suspected to herself...

"Ryane took deep breaths as they drove into the church parking lot. She looked at her new diamond watch and knew services would start in a few minutes. Jackie patted her hand and told her she was going to be just fine. She would also be in service since she had already arranged for someone to teach her class that day. With heads held high, the friends walked in and entered the side her family sat on. Todd met them, gave Ryane a hug, and then escorted her down the aisle. She nodded to those who caught her eye with her focus on keeping one foot in front of the other until she saw her mother. She rushed into her opened arms.

"Mommy," she whispered as she fought back the tears. Seeing her brought the baby out of her. They held on to each other as if this was going to be their last time seeing one another. Both grandmothers were standing and awaiting their turn. "Grandma, Nanny." She gave them both strong hugs and gentle kisses. "I've missed you all so much." Her daddy and grandfathers had made their way to where they were standing. Now in her daddy's arms, she couldn't contain her tears any longer. He walked her to one of the side doors. They entered the corridor which led to the fellowship hall. Her mother and grandparents followed.

"Was that Ryane?" Justin asked his friend, Todd.

"Yes and—"

They were interrupted.

"Justin, they said my sister is here. Ryane came home. Where is she?"

"Rena, calm down, she's with your parents and grandparents in the fellowship hall," whispered her husband trying not to bring attention to them.

"I want to see her," she exclaimed, rushing out of the door down the hall.

Justin grabbed her before she entered the room.

"Baby, wait, that's not a good idea."

She tried to pull away and became hysterical. "I want to see my sister…Please, let me see my sister…Let me tell her I'm sorry." She began sobbing her name over and over…"Ryane…Ryane…I'm sorry…I'm sorry…please forgive me."

Justin held on to her for dear life. He couldn't take the chance of Ryane striking her; she was five months pregnant.

Ryane heard her and pulled out of her Pawpaw's arms.

"Ryane, wait," said her grandma. "Son, don't let her out!" She saw a dangerous expression of evil and sensed her hostility. Something she had never seen or felt with her grandbaby. Her Ryane was kind, loving, compassionate, and forgiving.

Her father tried to grab her, but she was faster than

an Olympic sprinter. When Justin saw her, he immediately tried to shield his wife with his body, but not before Ryane was able to get one good slap across her face. Whether it was the lick from her sister or her husband's shove, she lost her balance completely. While their Pawpaw and the women rushed to Rena, the others tried to pull Ryane off of Justin. She was using all her limbs viciously, not sparing any mercy. He was receiving brutal, painful blows. The women screamed "Get her...get her!" The men were having a difficult time corralling her. Her behavior was that of a deranged person attacking Justin with all her might, deaf to the pleading of her stunned parents and grandparents. They had never witnessed this kind of behavior. Todd grabbed and lifted her completely off the floor, taking her into one of the private rooms. Jackie was right behind him.

Ryane was hysterical and beyond livid. She was enraged. Jackie felt terrible as she watched her best friend pace the small room, breathing hard like a vicious dog gone mad. She should have seen this coming. How many times had Ryane said all she had for her baby sister was a *bonified azz whupping*?

Todd stuck his head out the door to see how things were. The hall was now clear. They must have taken Rena to the ladies' lounge which was located on this side. He looked at Ryane and then Jackie. His baby shook her head for him not to say a word. He walked over to the small refrigerator and took two waters out. Ryane refused hers. He took it instead and continued to stand guard on the door. He wasn't taking any chances. Someone tried to enter, but not with his three hundred-pound body leaning against the door. He opened it with her peering over to the side, waiting to see who was coming in. It was her

120

parents. Her mother spoke first.

"Ryane, what possessed you to hit your pregnant sister? I know you're hurt, but to physically do bodily harm to your pregnant sister. You should—"

The deadly glare she gave her mother stopped her cold, sending terrifying shivers through her body. Beverly Newton didn't know who this woman was, standing in front of her. She was totally out of character. Certainly wasn't her beautiful, sweet, adorable first born. This woman was hard, mean-spirited, and plain cruel. Justin's face was scratched up worse than the first time, and poor Rena was distraught and heartbroken. All she wanted was her sister.

"I should what, Mother?"

Her mother just shook her head, wiping her tears. For the first time as a mother, she was afraid to speak her mind and looked toward her husband. After all, she was a daddy's girl.

He walked over to her and spoke softly. "Come here, baby."

She walked into his embrace with a trail of tears on her cheeks, repeating *she was not sorry*. And he believed her as he felt and caressed her trembling body. The core of her entire soul was consumed with hate and anger.

Nanny came in to give them a report on Rena who was on her way home with Justin and his mother. Her doctor wanted her on complete bed rest for the next forty-eight hours. "I told her we would stop by and check on her after service, Ryane."

"No, Nanny, I'm going home." She left her father's

embrace and moved closer to the door.

"Ryane, this is your home," said her father sorrowfully. She was breaking his heart.

"No, Daddy, I can't stay here. And I'm sorry for embarrassing you, mother, and the family. I know I was raised better, but I'm in a difficult place in my life right now. I'm ashamed to admit I'm struggling, trying to be the woman you and mother raised. I wish everyone would understand how I feel."

That brought tears to her father's eyes. Not only was his heart broken, he was also losing his baby. His mother walked over to console him.

"Ryane, believe us, we do," said Nanny. "We all know what Rena and Justin did was a terrible thing. But it's done, and you must resume your life. You can't continue allowing hostility to fester and take over your spirit. You're too beautiful of a person to let other people's sin rob you of your personal joy and peace, especially now." Now...what was Nanny saying? Did she know already?

"Nanny, it's obvious I can't handle being here. I tried and look what happened, I lost complete control."

"Ryane, do you hate your sister?"

She turned to face her grandma, who had been quiet through the entire ordeal. "No, Grandma, I don't hate her, but—"

"No buts, Ryane," she said softly as she walked up to her.

122

"Grandma, what about me and how I feel? I'm the victim here."

She embraced her precious granddaughter tightly against her bosom, smoothing out her curls that sprung back each time. "Yes, you are, baby, but just like Lavinia said, you've got to let this go. Don't let their past sin keep your heart and soul bound with your life behind a stop sign. You're allowing two people who are remorsefully sorry with penitent hearts steal your joy and godly spirit. Trust me, baby, that's not what they want you to do."

"Grandma Daisy is right, Ryane. Poor Rena is —"

"Poor Rena, Mother, I don't want to hear anything about poor Rena! It's all her fault!" Ryane turned and glared at Jackie who knew she was done.

"Todd, bring the car around to this side."

Ryane looked at her family with sadness and regrets. She couldn't help thinking she should have followed her first mind and stayed in Allanville. At least she wouldn't have given their church family something else to talk about. She deeply regretted adding more pain and shame to her undeserving parents and grandparents. But what was done was done as Nanny said. Nonetheless, Rena was finally able to feel her wrath, and Justin got a taste of her crazy side once again. According to Jackie by way of Todd, that was what he'd called her behavior.

"Baby, don't leave," begged her mother with her daddy wanting to express the same sentiments but he was too emotional to speak. This was his first born, who wore his name, getting ready to walk away from her family. He knew only death would bring her back and *Lord* knows none of them wanted that, including her.

"I must, Mother, and I can't begin to say how sorry I am for... for..." Ryane couldn't continue and just repeated her sentiments with her mind saying they could take it anyway they wanted to. "I sincerely hope you all can salvage the rest of this day. I'll call you tonight, Mother. Now go check on Rena and her baby. I love you all."

"Ryane, what about worship?" asked her Nanny. "We were at the first service, but you?"

Leave it to Nanny, she thought and forced a smile. "Nanny, it's okay." When she saw Todd at the door, she went around and hugged her family. Her Pawpaw asked could they at least have family prayer before she left. She nodded, yes. A circle was formed and he prayed a heartfelt prayer with tears dropping. Afterwards, she exited through the side door...

Before going to the airport, Todd pulled up at one of the sister churches and told her she was not getting on a plane without worshipping first. She and Jackie both fixed her hair and make-up and they went inside, taking back seats. Minutes later the minister mounted the pulpit...

After service, Jackie tried to pressure her into having lunch. Ryane insisted she didn't want to go anywhere but to the airport and would grab a sandwich there. She had taken up enough of their day and would be forever thankful for their support. They said their tearful goodbyes for now with Ryane disappearing into the terminal. All she wanted to do was change her clothes and get something to eat...

"Sistah, that's a bad suit you wearing."

124

"You think so?"

The attendant nodded a yes.

"Are you a mother?"

She held up three fingers.

"If you wait a minute, I'll give it to ya."

"For real?" asked the lady.

"Really," said Ryane, "and happy Mother's Day!"

"Thanks, Sistah, you've truly made it just that. My kids are too young to buy me a gift and *Lord* only knows where their father is. And at this time of my life, I don't care. It's just me and my three babies that I work hard for. I thank *God* for them every day. They keep me grounded and sane."

Ryane took all but twenty of the cash she had and placed it in the bag on top of the suit so she would know it was there. They were now announcing her flight; she gave the lady a hug and exited the ladies room.

*

Ryane called her parents once she'd had a warm bath and dressed for bed. She knew tonight she would drop off to sleep due to exhaustion but was blessed with a clear, peaceful mind. You would think she would have had a headache since her day had been extremely stressful with all the drama that she caused, this time. That was not so; she felt vindicated, relieved, and hopeful. She was thankful Todd insisted she worship before flying out. The sermon was uplifting and encouraging. Oh, she had no intentions of going home anytime soon, nor was she going to talk to Rena and Justin. However, she sent a text stating they were forgiven and hoped she and the baby were fine. After all, she wanted to be forgiven by *the almighty,* especially for her actions earlier. But most of all, she was not going to let them steal her joy any longer. She had a baby to think about now, because her Nanny said so even before she took the test. Nanny was always right.

On the way home, she stopped to get two reliable pregnancy tests and called Shelly to be with her. She was there when she drove up with a Mother's Day dinner the men in her family had prepared, which was well appreciated. They both shared the events of their day after the test. Shelly insisted they do that first, even before eating. They did and Ryane was pregnant and had the nerve to have mixed emotions. Humph, it was too late for that, scowled Ryane. Besides, the lady in the airport was her inspiration and she was thankful their paths crossed. Ryane told Shelly about her and their short conversation. What she said along, with her grandmothers' words, was imbedded in her mind. She was now ready to move on with her life.

Shelly told her she was glad she wasn't there to witness that drama, but more so happy to hear she was moving on. She stressed she really hoped everything was out of her system, because she now had the baby to think about. Ryane assured her it was. But she was honest enough to admit what she knew was the obvious truth. She didn't know when she would be able to look her sister and brother-in-law in the face without a small amount of disgust or a twinge of anger. Ryane also promised her family she would work hard on her disposition and certainly

126

keep her hands to herself. She just wished she could have said she was sorry for hitting her pregnant sister, but at the present time, she couldn't lie because she wasn't.

CHAPTER FOURTEEN

"Of course, Mr. Jenkins, I can see you and your event planner in twenty minutes. Have you had lunch?

"No, I'm afraid not."

"Good, I can order you something. Anything you have a taste for?"

"No, Ms. Newton, whatever you order will be fine with me." Ryane listened as he disconnected, and called down to the dining room. Wow, she was finally getting the opportunity to meet the Bailey *Bubba* Jenkins, the third proprietor and Nancy Tolliver, Allanville's prominent event planner. As she ordered two platters, which included an assortment of meats and sides, she checked her appearance. She was pleased she had added a long designer scarf to her cap-sleeved, black sheath dress this morning...

"Again, Mr. Jenkins—"

The handsome man gave her a friendly smirk.

"I mean, Bubba, we'll have everything set up to your liking."

"That's better. I'm sure you will, and remember, spare no expense for my beautiful bride." Bubba Jenkins also insisted on having a bill in spite of him being a partner. "Nancy?"

"I have a few more details to go over with Ryane, Bubba, you go ahead. I'll meet you at the shop later to give you the rest of the particulars."

Ryane locked her office door and was ready to leave for the evening. Today had been a good day, with tomorrow promising to be even better. She was having her first big VIP affair, which was a wedding in the hotel's beautiful rose garden and was expecting about a hundred fifty guests... Allanville's who's who. The day before, Bubba Jenkins had proposed to the love of his life who happened to be his best friend. They decided there wasn't a need for them to wait. And so, around sunset, they were going to have a simple ceremony...on a big Tuesday evening, sparing no expense. A splendid, practical idea, thought Ryane. What was the use in waiting? Maybe if she had done so instead of being engaged for five months, she would be Mrs. Justin Conners instead of her sister. There wasn't any need of pondering over what could have or should have taken place at this late date. Thanks to her sister, it was taken out of her hands, with her also being humiliated before the entire community.

*

Everything was ready for the bride, Trisha Johnson, and her best friend who happened to be the minister's wife, Jetta Brinkley. Ryane had seen them on Sunday mornings but never up close since she left right after collection. This was the first time she would actually face them up front, she thought while waiting for their arrival.

"They're here, Ryane," texted her assistant.

She walked out to the lobby to welcome them

personally. Ryane wanted to provide a personal touch from management. The friends were escorted inside. She greeted them with her beautiful smile, and introduced herself although her badge said she was the hotel manager. Both ladies accepted her firm handshake as they studied her. She was sure they were trying to figure out who was she related to. That was how it was in a small town. But she knew she didn't resemble anyone they knew. When Trisha inquired about her family, she said she was a distant cousin of Dexter Simpson by marriage, and was not from Texas. Ryane then accompanied the two friends to the elevator. They stopped on the top floor, which was the VIP suite. She unlocked their door and escorted them in. Both ladies were floored as they eyed the exquisitely decorated room with a fabulous bouquet of roses on a table set for two.

"Ladies, you will both have a complete body massage and facial." Ryane continued to give the duo their agenda for the rest of their beauty treatment. She told them a snack tray had been prepared with an assortment of beverages for their enjoyment. They looked at each other then back to her. A knock caused them to turn their gaze to the door, "Excuse me for a minute." She opened it, with a parade of people entering. "Good, everyone is here. Set the tables up in here, please."

Two men moved furniture while two women set up their trays as another followed the bellman to the bedroom. They were sure she was going to hang up their clothes for the wedding.

"Ms. Newton, are those tables durable?"

She flashed her beautiful smile. "Ms. Johnson, believe me, they are quite durable. They were purchased with people like us in mind." She winked and continued with her instructions. "Ladies, Esmeralda will be your personal attendant until you leave for the wedding. Now, if there's anything you need, feel free to call me. We want you to have a pleasant afternoon. Let me offer my congratulations, Ms. Johnson, you're a very lucky woman."

"Thank you, Ms. Newton for everything."

"It's my pleasure, Ms. Johnson. You two have a wonderful afternoon."

The ladies looked at each other silently agreeing there was a hidden sadness behind her professional smile.

*

"Shelly, you should see the rock on that woman's finger. Are you coming back to the wedding?"

"Yes, I'm on senior citizen's detail."

The ladies giggled and ordered a late lunch. While waiting for the waiter to bring it, Ryane asked about Nancy Tolliver. She was impressed with her professionalism and skills. More importantly, she wanted to talk to her about contracting her as an event planner for the hotel. It could be on commission while they continued expanding their services. Bubba and Trisha's wedding was another plus for the hotel's portfolio. Shelly told her that Nancy and the women in their family organized most of the special events

131

in their small town and would probably be interested. Ryane made a mental note. There was a knock on the door.

"Lunch," they both said together.

Ryane had pulled the drapes back so they could enjoy the beautiful view even if there was lots of activity going on for tonight's event. While they enjoyed their lunch, Ryane could tell something was on Shelly's mind.

"What's on your mind, friend?"

"How can you tell?"

"You're playing with your food," replied Ryane. Shelly put her fork down and looked at the woman she'd become attached to. "Go ahead, just say it, Shelly."

"According to Vic, Chancey sent flowers and a gift certificate to his mother and stepmother. And some were also put on his grandmothers' graves."

"Okay, meaning?"

"Meaning, I just wanted you to know."

"Look, Shelly, I thought we had been through this and named it what it was, a *booty call*."

"That's before you found out you're pregnant. By the way, when are you going to make an appointment to see the doctor? You know prenatal care is very important, especially in the developmental stages."

132

"I have one Thursday of next week for nine."

A smile spread across Shelly's face.

"I'm glad you're pleased, godmother."

"Me?"

"Of course, you're all I got. I haven't said anything to my family, only Jackie. I'm waiting until after my appointment for medical confirmation."

"Smart girl," Shelly received a text, it was the other clerk in her office. "I need to go Boss Lady. I'll see you tonight."

*

Ryane checked herself in the mirror before leaving her office. She had freshened up and changed into a faux wrap, royal blue dress with a double ruffle for sleeves and around the neckline. She adorned herself with pearl jewelry and a pair of strappy sandals the same color as her dress. She wanted to look her best and represent since this was a VIP's affair. As she entered the lobby, you could hear the smooth sounds of the local high school's combo playing soft jazz for Trisha and Bubba's wedding. She met Shelly and her entourage of senior citizens. They spoke and traded compliments. Everyone looked real nice with Shelly being her bold and glamorous self. They exchanged winks of approval and then Shelly escorted her family inside.

Ryane met Trisha Johnson and her group as they exited the elevator. "Ms. Johnson, you're truly breathtaking," she complimented with a hidden twinge of sadness.

"Thank you, Ms. Newton. I didn't know the hotel had a jazz combo?"

"We don't but I'm sure after tonight, we will. Your family and friends have enjoyed themselves immensely. Now I have proof to convince the proprietors it would be beneficial to have one. I hope you will find everything to your satisfaction."
Trish couldn't see what was outside for the drawn drapes in the lobby, but she was sure it was awesome and told her so.

"Ms. Newton, if it's anything like what I encountered earlier today, I know I will be quite pleased. Thank you so much for making this day perfect."

Ryane gave her a smile and Nancy took her hand to lead her to her awaiting family. Time was of the essence since they were using the sunset as the setting for the ceremony, which was such a romantic and thoughtful idea. Bubba Jenkins did this, Ryane thought. The love he had for Trisha was obvious. She couldn't help thinking she thought she had that once upon a time. As if that situation wasn't enough, she gave herself a wedding gift without a ceremony and now had a receipt. And her baby's daddy was now missing in action.

CHAPTER FIFTEEN

"Captain, I'm depending on you to get the rest of my men to safety, that's an order," panted Colonel Beasley.

"Colonel, please don't make me leave you, sir. We can manage, and we'll all get out together."

Black Thunder signaled for him to move closer so he wouldn't have to strain. "Swirl these men have families. We owe them, and we can't take the chance of overloading the aircraft. The wounded must get to the states. My injury is not critical, and I'll catch the next one after the storm."

Swirl knew what was important but not at Thunder's expense. He just didn't see it that way. The operation was a success with few fatalities. It was assumed Jackol and the rest of his men were killed in the explosion. Needless to say, they should have been home by now. But it didn't happen that way, thanks to Thunder, who couldn't shake his gut feeling of Jackol still being alive. And he was, along with five of his men. They were responsible for blowing up the resort, attempting to fake their own deaths. But thanks to Thunder's sixth sense, he had another plan in place. They were apprehended as soon as they swam to the boat they had stashed, not knowing it had been confiscated at the beginning of the operation. After all the planning and danger they'd endured, the island was now being hit by tropical storms, making it impossible for another rescue craft until after the severe weather passed. *Mother Nature* was now against them. They sent the wounded first, Jackol and what was left of his army, second. The last aircraft that made it through had limited space. The issue now was the island being overtaken by water. Sacrifices had to be made. They had already moved up to a higher point to safety for the time being, but nothing was promised, the water was constantly ascending with the dangerous winds. According to their rescue team, a hurricane was on the rise. Thunder should have left with the wounded, but he claimed it was not serious.

"Colonel, you're hurt more than you led me to believe, and you need medical attention."

"Captain, everyone is on board. We got to get out of here; the water is coming in fast."

"Okay, Lieutenant, go ahead, I'm on my way."

"Swirl, don't worry about me, I'll be waiting for your return. Remember, you have someone and maybe a baby on the way. Now, go!"

Chancey McGowan saluted his Colonel one last time and had turned to walk away when he heard him whisper, "I love you man, be safe and happy."

When he arrived, everyone was buckled up and ready to take off, all of them watching the giant waves. He didn't care if the chopper was already holding past regulation weight. They still could have made room for one more, thought Swirl as he secured parachutes with care packages. He had a plan, and with the grace and help of the *Almighty,* he and the Colonel would make it out of this hell hole.

"Lieutenant, you have your orders; now get this bird outta here, and good luck."

"To you, too, sir, and I won't let you down," he said, holding up the piece of paper he had in his pocket.

"I know you won't."

Thunder couldn't believe his eyes, then too, he could. They'd been together for a long time. Nobody was a better man to have your back than Chocolate Swirl. He loved him like a brother.

"What took you so long?"

They both exchanged sheepish grins.

"I had to get care packages and medical supplies for you. We don't know how long we're going to be stranded. I want to be prepared for whatever we have to endure. Now, let's move up as high as we can in this cave and sit this storm out."

"Swirl, I can't move a muscle. Can we have a minute?"

He watched his long-time friend close his eyes. "Naw, now get cha lazy azz up."

His eyes popped open.

"And don't try pulling that ranking *chitilians.*"

*

"Well, Ms. Newton, your suspicions are correct, you

137

are pregnant," Dr. Jamie Holly stated with a smile on her face. "I hope this is delightful news."

Ryane looked at her. "I'm not going to lie or try to fool you. I do have mixed emotions, but I'm okay. I've been looking forward to being a mother for some time. I just wish I hadn't bought the carriage...before the horse," they both said together, and laughed.

"Good, it's important to have a pleasant attitude during pregnancy. It makes it much easier. Since you were able to give me an exact date of conception, we're looking at a *Christmas* baby. Naturally, few women deliver on their due date, but it's important to have an idea to provide the best prenatal care. Do you have any questions for me at this point?"

Ryane shook her head, no.

Dr. Holly gave her what she called her goodie bag with everything for a new mother...prescriptions for prenatal vitamins and morning sickness, three pieces of literature on pregnancy, and a diary. The cutest little curly-headed baby girl was on the cover.

"Dr. Holly, she's just a little doll with those fluffy cheeks and arms."

"Well, thanks," she said proudly.

"She's yours?"

"Yes, ma'am, that's my bundle of joy at three months. She's six years old now."

138

Ryane exchanged more niceties with the doctor and exited the examining room. She stopped at the receptionist's desk to schedule her next appointment.

*

"Ice, sweetheart, we've covered the entire perimeter of this area that's on the paper, there's no sign of life."

"Diamond, I refuse to believe Swirl and Thunder are gone. Together those two can defeat Satan, himself."

"You're right, but they are nowhere on the island or fifty yards of the area. I need you to call off this search."

"I can't call it off. Because of the storms, we're already days late."

"Ice, you had no control of the weather. You even came out when everyone else said you were crazy after the storm was predicted to turn into a full-fledged hurricane. You've done all you could, now it's time for you to accept the fact they're probably—"

"Don't you dare utter those words to me, I will never accept that." Ice grunted harshly between clenched teeth.

Diamond stroked and patted her husband's back, which was her signal to let him know he was being unreasonable. "Let's compromise. We call it a day since it's late, return tomorrow."

Ice looked at the love of his life, "I'm indebted to them, baby. I owe those guys my life. If it wasn't for them, there would be no us and him," he said, pointing at her small baby bump. His tone was now softer as he caressed her gently...

"Listen, man that sounds like a chopper" yelled Thunder.

Swirl raised his head and mumbled, "I'll go check." Slowly standing on his weak legs, he didn't know who was worse off, him or Thunder. A few days ago, he was the one who thought a chopper was in the area and went running in the water, yelling to the top of his voice and waving his arms. All he got was a cold, a terrible cough that he couldn't seem to shake, and a sore chest.

"Man, you're in no shape."

"You just stay put." Swirl didn't have the strength to run this time. With the use of a stick for support, he walked as quickly as he could to the cave's entrance and shot the flare gun three times. He prayed the whole time that this was it.

"Sgt. Ice, I see something," shouted one of their men. Chocolate Swirl, thought Ice, grinning while instructing Diamond to take the chopper down.

*

Ryane sat at her desk caressing her stomach with thoughts of it getting bigger in a few months. She'd always had a pouch; it was just smaller after she dropped sixty

140

pounds. Since she'd been in Allanville, she'd gained ten of those pounds back and didn't care that she was back over the two hundred mark. She was always going to be a two hundred-pound girl, which was something she had accepted. Anyway, Nanny always said she took after the women on her side of the family. According to her, they were healthy, child bearing women.

Gazing out at the patio, her mind wondered back to the Jenkins wedding and how they were bubbling over with happiness. The unity rope ceremony was very unique, and it was the first time she'd witnessed one. They now had several weddings scheduled, starting with the current month until late summer. Nancy accepted her offer to become the hotel's part-time event planner. Shelly said that ever since Bro. Tyson became the new minister at the Allanville COC, he'd grown the church with young adults. A single's group was developed and had been quite successful. The Allanville Matchmakers, as they were affectionately called, had truly been on their job. As a result, young adults were meeting, dating, falling in love, and getting married. Shelly suggested they join. It would give them a chance to meet some eligible men and have some fun. After all, what did they have to lose? Ryane told her she should join, but she wasn't interested. A man was the farthest thing on her mind. She meant what she said about not getting involved.

Besides, she was with child and didn't need the complication. It was enough trying to keep her mood pleasant, especially since Chancey McGowan had disappeared off the face of the earth. She didn't care where he was and who he was with. All she wanted to do was let him know she was pregnant, but so be it. He'd just find out whenever he decides to stroll back into town. Shelly told her his people were also concerned. Chancey had never stayed away this long and not give his family a courtesy call. But they didn't know what the friends knew. He and some woman by the name of Diamond were together, according to what Ryane and Shelly overheard at the concert. Ryane had made up her mind she would still have a talk with his grandfather to give him the news. However, she would make it clear she did not want anything, just wanted him to know about the baby before she came.

Humph, wishing in vain, Ryane thought. With her luck it would be a boy with his daddy's looks. That should have put a smile on her face, but it didn't. She was naïve enough to think she could have one baby's daddy; what a crock. With Chancey playing his disappearing act, she would have to find another, and then too, one child may have to be enough. Who was she fooling? She didn't want another man to touch her. Ryane was like the other women in line, now she understood why. Her body craved for some Chocolate Swirl, only, and she couldn't wait to request another booty call.

*

"What cha doing, girl?

"Oh, just *chillin*. How was your date last night?"

Shelly sighed.

"Surely it wasn't that bad."

"On the contrary," replied Shelly. "To be honest, I

had a wonderful time, but I don't know about Dennis Randal. He seemed preoccupied."

"What makes you think that?"

"He kept looking at his watch."

"Didn't you say he lives with his grandmother? Maybe he was just concerned about her. You of all people know what senior citizen's detail is like."

They both giggled, because she did and thanked her friend for reminding her.

"So tell me, do you like Mr. Randal?"

"The question is whether he likes me. You know there's an age difference, although I don't have a problem with that."

"Really, Shelly, this is your third date, so it can't be an issue for him either.

"Unh-uh, second," Shelly said between taking sips of her drink. "The first one didn't count since it was at the church."

"Whatever, he's the one who did the asking."

"Yes he did, and kissed me good night this time. Girl, I believe he was trying to sneak a feel on my boobies; he held me so tight. And yes, he felt and smelled good."

"So are you and Mr. Randal going out tonight after work?"

"No, tonight he invited me over. He's going to cook dinner."

143

"Wow, how sweet."

"I thought that was kind of nice, too."

"What are you going to do tonight?"

Ryane told her she was going to clean her place and make flight reservations for Father's Day weekend. She decided to spend the entire weekend, thanks to her best friends' encouragements. They didn't hesitate to remind her how lucky she was and not to take her father for granted. Both lost theirs at a different time in their lives. Jackie after she finished college and Shelly when she was a mere teenager. Ryane made her mind up then that she would not miss any holidays with her parents, in spite of her sister and brother-in-law. While Ryane told Shelly her plans to fly out Thursday night, Shelly received a text from Vic.

"Ryane, hold up a minute Vic is sending me a text." She read it aloud. It was about Chancey McGowan. *Diamond called Judge / Chancey in hospital / pneumonia / Get back 2 ya…*

"Now you know why he hasn't been home or called."

"Shelly, did you read the message right? Vic said the same name we heard at the concert, **Diamond**… she must be his main woman."

"Okay Ryane, I hear ya, and I have to admit I'm disappointed in that Chocolate Swirl, and don't you dare say it."

"What, he was only a booty call?"

"Bye girl, I need to get cute for my dinner date."

Ryane swiped her phone and went into her kitchen to wash the few dishes and take care of the remainder of her house cleaning chores.

CHAPTER SIXTEEN

Humph, Ryane was disappointed in Chancey McGowan, herself. She also prayed he was okay, even if he did have a special woman. It was her Christian duty and she was carrying his baby. *Yeah, right, screamed her conscious. You have the hots for that man.* Her entire body and soul yearned for him...her eyes for his glorious, chocolate physic with that little swirl of cream...her nose for his sexy masculine aura...her lips for his intoxicating kisses...her ears for his spellbinding voice...and her skin for his sizzling, tender touch...Is this how it was going to be since she decided to be a link on his chain and have his baby? She couldn't believe she was that naïve thinking that he wouldn't be a part of her thoughts twenty-four seven. It was not because she was having his baby either, that was what she wanted. Maybe this was part of her punishment for the way she went about getting her bundle of joy, and most of all, for lusting after that Chocolate Swirl. One thing for sure, this was not going to be an easy job. *Ryane, Ryane what have you done?*

*

The McGowan family had finally received word concerning Chancey and his whereabouts. He and Thunder were in pretty bad shape when they arrived in Brownsville two weeks earlier. In the end, Swirl had been worse off than Thunder. The doctors marveled at his strong constitutional will. It was amazing; while his health was failing, he still managed to take excellent care of

Thunder. But Chancey, on the other hand, contracted pneumonia, with one of his lungs collapsing once they arrived. It was touch and go for a few hours, but he pulled through. The doctors assured his family and friends the worst was over. He was out of danger and would be good as new in a few days. They kept him on strong antibiotics and administered breathing treatments. For the first week, his communication was limited. Nothing above a whisper with him constantly expressing that he wanted to go home.

Swirl was restless and agitated about something. Although his family didn't have a clue, Thunder did. Ryane Newton. And he wasn't going to rest until he got home to see her. She had been his entire conversation for weeks until he started feeling poorly. His sleep was consumed with her, dreaming and constantly calling out to her. When Thunder confronted him about being in love with Ryane, he tried to deny it. He then admitted it was true, he loved her but it was complicated. His grandfather had made it clear she was off limits. Nonetheless, his boy asked him to keep what he revealed between the two of them.

In spite of all that they'd been through, their recovery was remarkable and they would be a hundred percent. Thunder was released Monday, but decided to stay with Chancey. Father's Day didn't mean anything to him. Ice and Diamond were also waiting around to see if they were going to release him that day since there had been talk of doing so...

"Doctor, can we take him home?" asked his father. The family felt he would do much better in familiar surroundings and in his own bed. Although he was improving physically, emotionally, his spirits were low. Home would be better.

"Mr. McGowan's recovery is remarkable, and we had planned to discharge him in a day or two. He's much stronger. Even his cough was improving and will continue to do so as long as he takes his medicine. However, we can't stress enough the importance of him getting adequate rest and nutrients or he will surely stand a chance of having a relapse. If you can promise to see that he does just that, we'll dismiss him right now."

Smiles spread across the family members' faces at the good news...

Chancey couldn't wait to get home and in his own bed even though he made promises that he had no intentions of keeping. All he could think about was his baby probably feeling he didn't care and had abandoned her. Not only did he care, he loved her until it hurt. The thought of never being able to make love to her was too much for even him. He was driven to survive the ordeal to make sure they were never apart again. All he wanted was to spend the rest of his life loving her and making her know how special she was to him. With a big grin on his face, he added more children to the equation...

"Shelly, this is Chancey...thanks...I'll feel better if I can get Ryane's cell number...yes I know she went home...thanks Shelly, I owe you. He didn't have any of her numbers and had called the hotel, but they said she was gone for the weekend. He should have known she would spend Father's Day with her father. She was a daddy's girl. But Shelly came through.

*

Ryane walked to the boarding area and took a seat. She still had another twenty minutes before they called her flight. Three times she'd started to just cancel, but didn't. She woke up this morning with her mind and heart heavily weighed. To say she was apprehensive and just plain nervous was an understatement. Although she was determined not to have a repeat of last month's drama, she still hated to face her family alone. With Jackie not going to be there, she didn't know how she was going to survive the weekend. She and Todd were going to his family's small Texas town to be with his grandfathers. Her support would have to be her cousins, who she'd avoided since the mess with Rena and Justin. Ryane would have to face them alone, which was causing her stress she didn't need. Her cell rang, and she looked at the caller ID. It was him! Shelly said he would be home today. Her lips began to quiver as she pressed the button to her earpiece.

"Hi, baby," greeted Chancey, and then he coughed a couple of times.

"Hi, yourself. How do you feel?" she said in a trembling voice.

He detected she was emotional but decided not to question her just yet. "Much better now that I hear your voice. You can't imagine how many times I wanted to call you. I've missed you so much."

God, she needed him, his strength and warmth, but knew that was wishful thinking. After all, she was just a link on his chain. Still, the woman in her had a twinge of jealousy and had to ask, "What about Diamond?"

She surprised him with her question, really caught him off guard. "How do you know about Diamond?"

She couldn't tell him she and Shelly went to the hotel hoping to see him to only find out he had a main woman. Nor did she want Vic's name to come up, but it was too late for that.

"I was concerned since I hadn't heard from you in weeks and called Vic. He said your lady friend Diamond had called to alert the family concerning your illness. I was sorry to hear that."

"Ryane, Diamond is not my lady. She's my good friend's wife and we're in the reserve together and part of a special task force. My lady, as you put it, would be the woman who's having my baby. It's you I care deeply for, Ryane Newton. The constant thought of you and our time spent together made it possible for me to survive the hell I've been through these last few weeks, along with the grace and mercy of *the Almighty God*. Just to have the chance to hear your voice and hold you in my arms again has been my driving force and strength. Believe that! Now, don't you have something to tell me?"

Her words were caught in her throat; she couldn't speak. Instead, she began to tear up with her heart racing, listening to his series of coughs. She wasn't expecting him to say how much she meant to him. Was he serious?

Silence, he knew she was digesting what he just said. "Ryane, better yet, save it until we see each other. Now tell me, are you going to be all right?"

"I have to be," she choked out. They were calling her flight. "Chancey, it's time for me to board the plane."

"I'll hold on until we lose the signal."

"Okay," she said softly.

"Ma'am, are you all right?" He heard the flight attendant ask and took out his other cell and texted his boy. He needed a favor in the worst kind of way.

Ryane shook her head, yes, and gave the concerned woman her ticket. She called his name but he didn't answer. Ryane could only assume they lost the signal. Well, at least he called and what he said was reason enough to give some serious considerations to them…

"Son, what are you doing? The doctors said for you not to exert yourself right off and get plenty of rest," pleaded his grandfather.

"I am and I will, Grandfather. But since you're here, I have something to tell you. Please have a seat."

CHAPTER SEVENTEEN

As Ryane entered the passengers' arrival area, she spotted her parents. She couldn't believe she was actually there after all the drama from her last visit a few weeks earlier. But here she was with plans to spend the entire weekend for the Juneteenth Festival. This had been a traditional Father's Day celebration for both of her families, with this year being special since both holidays were during the same weekend. They had planned a four-day camping trip with the whole *shebang* on the Newton's birthplace property that'd been kept in the family since slavery. One of her great uncles still lived with his son and family in the original old house that'd been modernized. Sunday morning after an early service, she would return home. This was going to be a test of her new attitude and disposition plus being with all of her cousins. Rena and Justin would also be present. She would do everything in her power to maintain control of her temper and most of all, keep her hands to herself. She didn't want to ruin Father's Day like she had Mother's Day. Then too, she might've done just that once she broke the news of her pregnancy. She'd keep to herself that it was a one night stand.

"Ryane," called her parents. She waved and walked into their embraces. It felt good being in their arms. She had missed them terribly. Daily calls just weren't enough. She needed to feel their warmth and love.

"Ryane, you look beautiful, baby," her mother said, giving her a big hug. "There's something different about you. Mother likes what she sees."

Her father expressed the same sentiments as he hugged her next and asked for her luggage claim ticket.

"Thanks, Mother and Daddy. You two look cute in your matching outfits." They had on jeans, red t-shirts with the family name in black, and cream hats. The family colors had been black and red for as long as she could remember. Instead of wearing the family t-shirt today, she decided to keep on her traveling clothes. The off-the-shoulder, red and black plaid tunic blouse and blue jean capris were airy and comfortable to sit out in the elements. She even had the top of her hair cut a little shorter so it would be that much more manageable. Comfortable shoes and gold earrings and bracelets completed her look.

"Baby, everyone is waiting for you. We're looking forward to having a great time." She knew her mother was feeling her out.

"Yes, Mother, I'm looking forward to a pleasant time, also."

"Great," said her daddy. "Let's hurry so we can beat the little traffic. We had to use Uncle Ray's truck. Junior and his wife were doing some last minute errands. And you know your Uncle Ray's truck may get overheated."

They all laughed because their uncle had lots of money but refused to buy a new vehicle. He said he didn't need one as long as his truck continued to crank up and get him where he wanted to go.

Ryane hated to put them through so much trouble, but her father insisted. The RV was already parked in their favorite spot on the camping grounds, and he didn't want to move it. But Uncle Ray's truck did just fine as they pulled onto the property. It was her who wasn't doing too well as her body began to tense. Her mother detected it right off. She patted her hand to assure her it was going to be just fine. Ryane could only hope so.

"Okay, ladies, we're here," announced her father as he stopped at the cart section. With emotions on edge, she watched her father retrieve his personal golf cart. Looking around, Ryane deemed the crowd was bigger than last year as she sat in the back seat. It seemed every year, more family members were participating.

As her father pulled up to the family's RV, Ryane took deep breaths to calm her jittery insides. Well, nothing has changed, she thought as she got out of the cart. Like always, the Newtons' and Alexanders' RVs were side by side in rows which made socializing between the two families much easier. Her mother thought it was best to tell her ahead of time that Justin's family would be there tomorrow. That wasn't a problem with her. She loved *her almost* in-laws. It was their son and brother who broke her heart along with her own sister. Getting off the cart, she thought, *well, here goes nothing, the big test.*

"Ryane," her name was echoed. She waved in every direction thinking she may as well get it over with. But first, she had to give her Nanny and Pawpaw, who were sitting in the front of their Winnebago with some of her relatives, a hug.

"There's our grandbaby."

154

Ryane walked right into their arms. Her Nanny whispered that she was glad her precious baby was back. She could feel her calm, compassionate spirit. Nanny just prayed it would remain once she set eyes on her sister. Her name was called again.

"Go on Ryane," encouraged her grandparents.

"We'll take care of your bag," said her parents.

She took out her cell and gave her purse to her mother, inhaled a deep breath, and began to stroll down the rows. She received hugs and kisses from family members on both sides, with lots of compliments on her new look. Naturally, some of her cousins couldn't believe she chopped all her hair off but had to admit she looked fabulous. She just wished she felt fabulous. This was a stressful ordeal, and that was the truth. Her daddy's two sisters gave her extra tight hugs while softly whispering how proud they were of her. They also expressed their admiration and love. She needed to hear that as she posed for pictures.

"Ryane." It was her first cousin, Lynn.

She turned to face her.

"Have you seen them?"

"No."

"Come on, I'll go with you. They are already sitting out front waiting for you at Grandma and Big Daddy's Winnebago. That's where we're having lunch." Lynn gave her an extra squeeze and could tell she was nervous. "Trust, we're all here for you."

"Grandma, she's coming this way," exclaimed Rena excitedly.

"Rena, you must calm down and remember what we've all said. Do not try to force yourself on her. And for God's sake, don't touch her."

"But Grandma, she's my sister; I love her."

"I know you do, baby, but you must give her time. And you have to think about your health and the baby."

Justin was looking at his very pregnant wife, praying she was listening to her grandmother. He didn't want a repeat performance of last time, and to make sure, he got up to pull his chair closer to her chaise.

Ryane greeted more family before she finally reached her mother's parents. "Grandma, Big Daddy," she said softly and walked into their welcoming arms.

"Ryane," mouthed Rena.

Justin took her hand in his and gave it a gentle squeeze. He could feel her trembles as she insisted on standing. He became uneasy and prayed a silent prayer as he helped her up.

Her grandparents kissed both of her cheeks and released her. Now, she faced the two people who caused her whole life to change. Surprisingly, with a strong confident voice, she spoke, "Rena, Justin, I trust you are both well."

"Oh, Ryane," said Rena, trying to walk toward her with Justin holding her.

Ryane backed away with her hands up. "Rena, please stay where you are," she said. The words came out a little rougher than she intended. To her surprise, no one uttered a word. No, she was not going to be physical, but she didn't want either one of them invading her space.

"Have you eaten, Ryane?" asked her Grandma, trying to ease the tension any way she could.

"No, but I'll get something down the line."

It was a known fact that most of the families prepared meals to their taste with enough to feed their families and visitors. She would just be a visitor; at least that was the notion she had until she glanced at her grandparents. Their sad expressions tore at her heart. But she didn't want to be in Rena's and Justin's company. Ryane didn't notice Lynn had already fixed their plates... fried catfish and shrimp, dirty rice, green beans, and pound cake. Big Daddy had also unfolded chairs for them.

"Daisy, I can smell that catfish. I hope it's as good as it smells," shouted her Pawpaw.

Ryane knew she had been set up when she saw her parents, and other family members following Pawpaw and Nanny who were walking toward them. So they were all in this together. She spoke...was polite...kept her hands to herself...but surely they didn't expect her to eat with them.

"Ryane, here, sit by me," Lynn said, patting a chair.

It was a conspiracy, she said silently, looking around at her family.

"Mmmm...Grandma, this dirty rice is *kickin,*" complimented Lynn.

Please, was on everyone's face, but her daddy said the actual words. "Please, baby."

For you only, Daddy, she thought and sat beside her cousin. Three of her other female cousins joined them once they served their families. They hadn't talked since everything transpired. She was sure they wanted to see how she really was, mentally and emotionally. Her parents sat by Rena which was understood. She didn't look well. Maybe it was due to the pregnancy. Ryane didn't have a clue since she had not allowed anyone to mention her name. And certainly did not want to know anything about her condition. Why should she be concerned about her after what she did? Humph, her conscious was probably giving her the bodacious whipping she deserved. Mmmm, Lynn was right, Grandma's dirty rice was delicious. As a matter of fact, everything was smacking good.

During the course of their meal, her family was quite talkative. Her cousins wanted to know about her hotel and how she was enjoying living in a town smaller than Texarkana. They also expressed how much they loved the new Ryane's hairstyle and look. The entire time, she felt Rena's stares, but not one time did she give her the satisfaction of making eye contact. Out of the corner of her eye, she saw Justin caress her large stomach and brush his lips against hers. It was obvious and couldn't be denied that they loved each other dearly. Ryane couldn't help thinking that maybe if they had gone about it another way...But what way was that? As her Nanny said, it was done, and she couldn't live a happy life dwelling in the past.

After cleaning up, Lynn suggested they take their evening stroll with her female cousins agreeing. Her Grandma tried to get her to stay. Ryane knew what she was trying to do, but it was not going to work. The less she was around them; the better her disposition would be for the moment.

"Grandma, we're going to tire the children out and let them ride their riding toys," stated Lynn. "We'll be back this way in a few minutes."

They all thought that was an excellent idea since their daddies were already engaged in their cards, dominoes, and video games. Her cousins had been holding their peace ever since Ryane came. They were all happy she didn't miss their celebration and most importantly, she was not going to alienate herself from the family because of what has happened. Naturally they couldn't wait to have some real girl talk, especially Darlene. They all knew Rena wanted to be involved, but she brought this upon herself.

CHAPTER EIGHTEEN

Once the cousins were out of earshot Darlene began with what she had to say. "Ryane, I'm going to say this one time, and I'm speaking for all of us. What Rena did was foul and almost unforgivable. But considering the way we were all brought up, we have to forgive and move on. Remember, it's not the end of the world. And judging from what we see, you've already figured that out and done just that."

Everyone agreed to what she said, echoing, *that's right*.

"Now, let's get to the good stuff...How was your first time and who is he?" asked Lynn.

Ryane stopped dead in her tracks and glared at the four women. Shaking her head with a smile, she should have known they would be able to tell; they were that close, being in the same age bracket. She was the only one still not married. They weren't as naïve as she was and guessed Rena wasn't either. Since they all decided to experience sex first and then marry, pregnant.

"Magnificent... Awesome... and Mind Blowing."

Girl-howls and whistles of approval were released.

"Okay, when's the baby due?"

Oh, Darlene wasn't leaving out anything, Ryane thought, giving her that "sistah girl" look.

"Girl, don't look at me like that. You know we're Nanny's girls. Need I say more?"

"Around Christmas, but please don't say anything. I haven't told my parents yet."

"Like Nanny ain't said something already."

"Darlene, you heard me."

She held her hands up and vowed they wouldn't hear it from her lips. "Now, tell us about him."

"To be honest, there's nothing to tell. He just happened to be around, and I hastily propositioned him. Basically, it was a one night stand and as you said, being one of Nanny's girls, I'm pregnant."

"Still, he must have been something special and extraordinary for you to give up your virginity," insisted Darlene.

Ryane was now smiling.

"Okay, cuz, give."

"It's just that he called my virginity *the Newton jewels*."

"Auh, that's sweet and cute; now tell us what's so special about this man," demanded Lynn.

"He's super-fine, savvy, and knows how to woo a woman with a mere smile...a bona fide, experienced player."

They all pretended to swoon as they turned around.

"And you like him a lot. Whether or not you're aware, your eyes change when you talk about him…bright and twinkling one minute, then dark and sensuous the next," said Darlene.

She was getting ready to deny it, but the glares she received said, *save it*. Ryane tried hard to convince them she was just one of the many links on his chain. How could she love someone like that? It was strictly physical. No one believed her and didn't hesitate to tell her. She hated being like the cover of a book you already know what's inside. Maybe if she hadn't expressed how sweet he was when he sent her a rose bush and chocolates, she would have been more convincing. Ryane now had a faraway look on her face as they continued their stroll.

"What are you thinking about?" asked Lynn.

"Girl, it's not what, it's who."

They all sang, *Chancey McGowan* and exploded with much laughter.

She pouted. "Ya'll laughing at me."

"No we're not, sweetie, we just know when a woman is in love. We've all been there and are still there," explained Lynn.

"But we've only known each other for a short time. And I just got out of a terrible relationship with a man I loved and thought loved me. It can't be love that soon. I believe it has more to do with me being plain horny and vulnerable at the time." Her voice sounded like she was asking more than telling.

162

"It's all three!" They shouted with laughter and high fives.

"Ryane, if you really give the relationship you and Justin had some serious thought, you would see it was lacking in more than trust. Justin was safe, predictable, and boring, if you ask me. You needed excitement and finesse. That's why he and Rena are perfect for each other, stick-in-the-mud preppies. You are a sistah girl. Can I get a *that's* right, girl," exclaimed Darlene.

That's right girl!

The cousins stopped their walk between their grandmother's and Darlene's RV. They decided to let the children ride back and forth for a while. They were already showing signs of fatigue. Before they could get comfortable, Grandma Daisy was waving them down.

"Ya'll, Grandma is not going to let us be until Ryane and Rena are in each other's company," said Lynn. "Come on, Ryane let's sit down there for a minute, then we can use the children as a scapegoat."

Darlene passed cold treats around and they strolled down to the next RV to please Rena. They were all sure she had put her up to it. Ryane warned them to change the subject or she was going inside. Somebody suggested they play cards which they all thought was a great idea.

Ryane wasn't really into cards, although she could play and had skills. But that was one thing she left behind in college. Plus, she was a sore loser unless it was Pluck. She could be plucked the entire time and was never upset.

They sat down to a game of Pluck and right off the

bat, she was plucked from all three ladies which brought about laughter and jokes. All of a sudden, there was a big commotion among the children.

"A helicopter, a helicopter," screamed the children, jumping up and down, pointing.

"That thing is flying mighty low," said Lynn. They were now all standing, calling the children while receiving much protest. "Don't look like it's coming any closer."

"Look, they're dropping a ladder," Darlene said as she shielded her eyes from the bright sun.

The menfolk had now appeared because the children were extremely excited as a man began to climb down with another following. Somebody asked if they were the police or something. The men were wearing combat attire and dark shades. A large bag was lowered. One of the men retrieved it and then they walked to the cart section. Everyone waited in suspense to see the direction they took. The duo soon stopped at the first row of RVs. A ringing sound caused everyone to check their pockets, each saying *it's not me*. It was Ryane's.

*

"Where are you, baby?"

To hear his voice and know that he was there caused her eyes to water. She stepped away from the crowd so he could see her. He was actually there…He had gotten out of his sick bed to be there for her.

"Can't be," said Darlene as the crowd watched the cart head in their direction.

It stopped, and an emotional Ryane rushed to the open arms of a smooth, dark-skinned guy that looked dignified in his combat gear. His face was mostly concealed with dark glasses and a cap, but not his trimmed mustache and dark, kissable lips.

"Stop your crying," he whispered and kissed her forehead, cheek, then lips.

The children sang, *auhhh*. The women had big grins on their faces while the men looked on. They held on to each other for what seemed like forever with her hiding her face in the bend of his neck and him squeezing her tight. She brushed her lips against his exposed skin as his cologne snaked up her nostrils. "All right, Rocky is also going to show you how much you were missed in front of your family."

Her parents and grandparents were now standing nearby.

"Sir," said the gentleman that came with him.

"Lieutenant Iceton, I would like you for you to meet Ryane Newton," he said, still holding on to her. He kissed her nose, which had already begun to spread a bit. She's going to be cute pregnant, he thought.

"Ms. Newton, it's a pleasure. My wife, Diamond, would like to speak to you," said the Lieutenant and gave her his cell. "Sir, you need to get off your feet."

"Lieutenant, I strongly suggest you get back to your wife," barked Chancey. He tried to take the cell from Ryane, and she gently pushed his hand away and walked him over to a chair. He nodded to her family and took a seat. She felt his forehead while she listened. Good, he didn't have a fever. He pulled his cap down on his face a little more and leaned his head back.

"I promise, Diamond, I will see that he does exactly what he's supposed to do and not exert himself. And thank ya'll for bringing him to me...I'll tell him...you two have a safe trip...goodbye." She gave the Lieutenant back his cell and told him to leave Chancey's bag next to the chair; she would take care of it. Ryane looked at her family, who remained in place as they watched. The two men saluted military style; Lt. Iceton left.

She introduced Chancey McGowan to her parents and grandparents first, and then to the rest of the family who had gathered around. He greeted them all with his mesmerizing smile and friendly handshake. She knew the women, including her mother and grandmothers, would be in awe of the debonair Chocolate Swirl and was enjoying the view. But she had to keep her promise. After the introductions, she asked her family to excuse them.

"I need to get him settled and get something in his stomach," Ryane said, taking his hand.

The question at the moment was whose RV they were going to stay in; certainly not with her parents. And she didn't want to be near her sister and brother-in-law. That meant Darlene's or Lynn's RVs.

No one noticed the man approaching. "We're looking for Captain McGowan," he announced. Captain was echoed among her family. And she looked at him in amazement.

"I'm Captain McGowan."

"Sir, we have your Winnebago. Where would like us to park it?"

"You bought yourself an RV?" asked Ryane.

"Nope, I bought us one; now where do you want it?"

One of the men asked where it was, and saw that a chocolate recreational vehicle with cream swirls that shouted mega bucks was parked at the entrance. A dream machine, thought her male cousins.

Lynn's husband, Jake, spoke for Ryane and told him to put it in front of the black and gold Winnebago. That was a great idea; that way the night's noise wouldn't disturb him while he rested since they were having a big crawfish boil with the works. Pawpaw gave him the keys so he could make room. Once the luxury vehicle was in place, they said their goodbyes for now and went inside. A few minutes later, her cousin came with their bags.

Her questioning expression caused Jake to give an explanation. "Uncle Ryan sent your bags, too, figuring you were staying with him. Man, this is what you call an RV," he said, looking around.

She couldn't stay under the same roof with him with everyone present...especially her parents and grandparents, or could she? It wasn't like they were going to have sex, he was sick.

"Oh, and Aunt Bev said she would send some gumbo soup for him in a few minutes. My brother, you need to lay down, you don't look so good."

Ryane and Chancy thanked Jake and watched him leave. He then gathered her in his arms to hold her close to his weary body. His face was a little warm. He nudged her neck and whispered he didn't know he could miss anyone so much as he did her. And he never wanted to be away from her that long ever again. He had to pull away quickly to cough. She watched him bend over, holding his stomach and asked, "You're in pain?"

"Just a little when I cough," he said and went to get his toiletry bag for his medicine. "Baby, will you please get me a bottle of water from the fridge? And after I take this, I think I'll take a shower."

She turned to do so and was surprised to see it stocked with not only water but other drinks along with the basics. He told her Diamond had the RV stocked with food and essential kitchen items. Ryane gave him the water and unzipped his bag.

"Baby, I'll do that after I've rested."

"No, you go ahead and take your shower while I unpack. But don't stay in there too long, you'll get over heated. Let me have your meds. You shouldn't take them on an empty stomach."

He gave her the medicine bag and went into the spacious shower. He was right about Diamond; she had provided everything he needed, he thought as he grabbed a towel.

CHAPTER NINETEEN

Ryane was just about done with the job of unpacking and putting their things in place when she heard a knock on the door. She knew it was probably one of her cousins with the gumbo soup. "Come in," she yelled from the bedroom. "I'll be right out." She walked into the living area and to her surprise, it was her parents. "Mother, Daddy."

"This is very nice, Ryane," her mother said as she put the large bowl on the marble counter.

"Honey, this is more than nice. This is the top of the line for a recreational vehicle this size. I wouldn't be surprised if this thing didn't have a bath and a half," her father said, opening a door. Sure enough, it did with a stackable washer and dryer.

Watching her mother walk around feeling the soft leather, she turned to her daddy who was now busy checking out the media center with a remote control in his hand.

Chancey turned the water off and heard voices. From what he could make out, her parents were questioning her about him.

"So, Ryane, tell us about Capt. McGowan, besides him thinking a lot of you," requested her Mother.

"What makes you say that, Mother?"

Beverly Newton became perfectly still as she looked at her beautiful, naïve daughter. "Baby, surely you don't think that man got out of his sick bed to fly here in a helicopter and buy this expensive RV because he just likes you. That man is in love with you. And I may add you have strong feelings for him as well, and I dare you to deny it."

Her father nodded his head in agreement as he glanced her way. He detected something special about this man whether she admitted it or not, with that starry-eyed look she was trying to conceal.

Chancey had a wide grin on his face. Mrs. Newton was a very wise, observant woman and had hit the nail on the head. He loved their daughter, and she would know just how much, he thought, putting the little black pouch in his pocket as he listened for her response.

"First of all, Mother and Daddy, we've only known each other four short months. And as far as this RV, Capt. Chancey McGowan is extravagant and buys only the best of everything," explained Ryane with emphasis on the word Captain. She couldn't get that out of her mouth good without her mother giving her the eye. Okay, they wanted to know the truth; she would tell them just that. She was sure nothing she said at this moment would shock them after Rena and Justin's deceitful act.

"We do have an understanding and will be sharing—"

That was his cue. Hearing the word, *sharing*, he walked out. Ryane was sure the expression on her face clearly stated the one thing they shared, but that was not what she was going to say. Dang, he was so sexy, looking

170

divine in a pair of soft, cotton pajamas with the shirt hanging open exposing his muscular chest and tattoo. Naturally, the words were snatched right out of her mouth with her being robbed of her very thoughts all at the same time. She was behaving like the other women on his chain in need of a Chocolate Swirl fix. As her friend Shelly would say, so stone her to death for admitting the truth.

"Baby, as you were saying, we'll be sharing?"

He was listening, she thought, looking from him to her parents then back to him. She saw a distinct smirk of a smile and knew he was enjoying the position she was in. His eyes also dared her to utter those senseless words she said to him in the beginning. She didn't believe them, then and he sensed she certainly did not now. Ryane knew all he saw was the yearning and longing for the man she wanted and loved.

God, only he could be so fortunate, Chancey thought as he waited for her to say what he already knew.

"Chancey."

"Yes, baby."

Oooh, she wished he would stop as she and her parents watched him invade her space.

"Mother and Daddy," she paused to look into his eyes for the strength and courage she knew he would give. "I'm pregnant, and Chancey and I will share the birth of a boy or girl around Christmas."

The room was so silent you could hear her expelling deep breaths of air.

171

"Thank you, baby," Chancey said, kissing her hand before taking her into his arms.

Her parents watched with smiles, their own private thoughts embedded in their minds.

"Girl, you've made me the happiest man on earth."

She looked at him and kissed his jaw. The feeling was mutual. Deep down inside, she expected that from him; he was going to make a great father. She wanted his baby and him, too. Ryane decided at that moment she would accept being a link on his chain as long as she came first with his women respecting her as his baby's momma.

She then looked at her parents, who still had smiles on their faces. "Mother and Daddy, I wish I could say I'm sorry."

Chancey walked toward the dining table to take a seat and coughed as they watched.

"Ryane, we can talk later. Right now you need to feed him so he can take his medicine and go to bed," said her Mother softly.

Dr. Newton told him to follow orders and get some rest. Chancey who couldn't respond for trying to hold in a cough, waved instead to acknowledge her father's comment...

"Okay, Chancey you need to get in bed."

She'd sat there long enough in pure agony, drooling over his naked chest, watching him eat and take his meds. She wanted so much to taste his chocolate swirl skin and nibble on his jelly bean nipples, but not now, she told herself.

"Ryane, I'm feeling better already," he said, sounding pitiful. "I haven't coughed once, and I ate all the gumbo soup. Which I might add, was delicious."

She looked at him with a smile. He was so cute, trying to convince her to let him go outside to mix and mingle with her family.

"Baby."

"Don't *baby* me, you need to rest. Now come on; let's go. After your nap, you can go to the crawfish boil."

He accepted that as something to really look forward to and allowed her to pull him into the bedroom. She picked up an extra box of tissue and hand sanitizer on her way. She sat it on the table made into the headboard along with another water and juice for him. Turning back the black and plum covers, she ordered him to get in.

"Baby, please stay with me for a while, at least until I fall asleep," he pleaded as he took off his shirt and patted the spot beside him.

She swallowed hard as he flexed his stiff shoulder muscles. She stroked his shoulder. That was a mistake, now she wanted to do more. But she felt the tensed tightness and knew he needed a massage more than her caresses. She pushed him gently down on the bed and told him to get on his stomach. Ryane straddled him so she could begin to work the tense kinks out of his muscles. Her firm, but tender, touch was what the doctor ordered, he thought as he moaned.

"Ryane," he called.

"Yes?"

"We need to talk about our baby and the new life we're going to have."

She paused for a second, and then resumed the task at hand. "We have plenty of time to talk about the baby," she said as her touch turned into caresses on his naked skin.

He noticed the difference right off. "Are you getting ready to take advantage of a sick man?"

"Exactly. You're sick, and need to get your strength back so we can play."

That produced a smile as he flipped over with her in his arms. She was now on top of him.

"You cannot rest like this."

"Yes, I can," he said, easing her top down.

Her strapless bra came down, too, with her breasts leaping out at him and her nipples beginning to stand at attention as the air hit them. She tried to push him away because she knew where this was going. All she needed was for everyone to hear her scream her head off.

"One quick suck is all I want baby, and then I'll stop. I got something important to ask you." He moaned as he took an erect nipple in his mouth and the other between his fingers.

She moaned right along with him and eased back on the pillow for his so-called one quick suck. He placed one of his legs between hers and began to work his hand down inside her capris. She knew it; her body trembled as he found the spot he knew would drive her completely over the edge. Again, she tried to stop him. He captured her hands and held them above her head and sucked in as much of her breast as he could while his magic fingers did their job. Her body twisted, her insides quivered as loud moans escaped from deep within. Being consumed by overpowering trembles and short jerks with each suck and stroke, Ryane tried desperately to hold in her screams. She felt the forthcoming of a turbulent climax.

"Ughhhhhh—"

He loved watching her climax and covered her mouth with his to silence her cries...

"Okay, that's enough for now," he said a few minutes later.

After she gained her wits, she tried to put her breasts back into the strapless bra. He wouldn't let her, using them as his pillow instead, kissing and caressing each one.

"What about you and Rocky?"

He leaned up with a slick grin and replied, "If everything goes according to my plans, we'll get ours later." With that, he put his head back on his fleshy, human pillow.

They began caressing each other when he asked the unexpected.

"Ryane, marry me?"

"Marry you," she repeated. "Chancey, don't you think it's too soon for marriage?"

"No, I don't," he said. "And baby, I don't want you to think about what has happened in the past. Let's move forward with just you me, a future together, leaving all the drama behind where it belongs. I don't want to live another day without you Ryane, I love you."

"You love me?"

"Yes, is that so hard for you to believe? Your mother has already told you."

"You were listening," she exclaimed, playfully hitting him.

"Of course I was," he admitted, half smiling with his eyes opening and closing.

"But."

"But nothing, just say yes, baby. One word, yes, is all I want to hear. As a matter of fact, I order you as the mother of my child."

She laid her head back on the pillow to rest.

Feeling the rapid beat of his heart, she asked, "Why is your heart beating so fast?"

He looked into her concerned face. "Ryane, for the second time in my adult life I'm afraid."

"The second time? When was the first time?"

Squeezing her with all his strength, he spoke. "When I thought I would never get to gaze into your lovely face, hold you in my arms, taste your sweetness, and watch you fall apart in my arms."

Just like she'd stated, he was just as good with words as he was at pleasuring a woman, leaving them mesmerized with both. Yep, she was definitely under the spell of Chancey McGowan. They switched positions and she caressed his naked chest and nipples.

"Yes, I'll marry you, Chancey McGowan, and it's not because I'm having your baby." She leaned up to look into his handsome face and said the words she never had any intentions of saying ever again. But she loved this man and wanted him to know she did. "I'm marrying you because I love you."

"Ryane," was all he was able to say.

She silenced him with a tender kiss.

"I have something for you."

"What?"

He pulled out the biggest round-cut diamond solitaire. She gasped as she held her hand out. "It's beautiful Chancey."

"It's for a beautiful lady. I also have something else for you. Look in the drawer where you put my things and get a red pouch and the brown envelope."

Ryane crawled to the end of the bed and opened his drawer to get what he asked for. He took out a gold bracelet that had a platinum charm with diamonds accenting the date she was supposed to have gotten married on. She looked at him for an explanation.

"I want you to remember March the twenty-first as a special day in my life. It's the day you stole my heart." A tear fell as he put it on.

She brushed her lips against his and placed her head back on his chest. "What's in the envelope?"

"Marriage license," he said, waiting for her next question.

"Marriage license, how did you manage that?"

"I had a few strings pulled just in case we run into problems. Is there somebody here that can marry us after I've had a nap?"

She should have known license would be his least problem with his grandfather being a retired judge.

"The only ministers here are Justin and his father. I wouldn't dare ask them. Although I love his family, I wouldn't want to put them in that position."

"Well, we can go to the justice of the peace in one of the nearby towns."

A smile spread across her face.

"What, you know somebody?"

"Yes, my great uncle is the justice of the peace for this area. He can do it," she said, admiring her new jewelry.

"You like your ring?" he asked with his eyes fluttering.

She kissed his chin. "I love it as much as I love you;

now you rest."

"Girl, I love you so much, and we're going to have a great life. Ryane," he stated softly.

"Mmmm," she moaned.

"It's a chance I may not be up to par with my performance tonight or for a few days due to the meds I'm taking."

"I know, but we can still have some grown folks fun and call each other's name.

He laughed. "Girl, you're a mess, but yes we can."

"Chancey, you don't have a wedding band."

"Yes, I do. I bought us both one when I purchased your ring."

"You thought of everything, didn't you?"

"I tried," he said, surrendering to the effects of his medicine and falling asleep.

She kissed his cheek and began to send text messages, then she got one... *c/u come out 2 pla w/ us now... lol* Ryane smiled because she knew what they wanted, and slipped away once he was in a sound asleep.

CHAPTER TWENTY

"Cousin, that man is *finnnne!*" exclaimed Lynn with everyone fanning themselves.

"Wait girls, look at that rock!" shouted Darlene. "Is this what I think it means?"

Ryane used her other hand to help hold up her ring hand as if it was that heavy. "That's exactly what it means. He said he loves me and want to spend the rest of his life with me and our children."

"Girl, I'm not the least bit surprised. The mere fact that man dropped out of the sky to get to you after leaving the hospital is proof enough. There should be no doubts with anyone."

The rest of her cousins agreed with Lynn.

"When are you going to do it?" Darlene asked.

"He wants to do it sometime tonight. And it will be private, of course. I hope y'all understand."

"Of course we do, Ryane," was echoed among them. And then they all wished her the best and told her to be happy.

"Oh, and put you a hand towel close by to muffle your screams," Lynn suggested. "Children will be camped outside tonight. They don't need to be frightened."

"Thanks for the advice, Lynn." Ryane looked at her

cousins and burst into laughter with them all giving high fives and hugs.

Nanny's dinner bell began to ring. They could hear Pawpaw shouting, "The crawfish boil is now open."

"Come on, Ryane, you know me and my family don't eat crawfish, either. Let's go to Mama's and Daddy's RV. They're having fried chicken, potato wedges, salad, banana pudding, and bread pudding."

"Mmmm, now you talking my kind of language," moaned Ryane. She and Lynn didn't believe in it.

"Don't forget your niece and nephew," shouted Darlene.

"We want crawfish!"

That settled that. Darlene took her two by the hand. "Tell my auntie to put my dessert aside. I'll be down there when I finish eating my crawfish."

When they arrived at her aunt's RV, the first person they saw was Justin and knew Rena couldn't be far.

"Lynn, I can't."

"Oh yes, you can," said her cousin, grabbing her arm with them marching right into the camp.

"Ryane, come and sit. I knew you would be here sooner or later. I already put your chicken and salad in a carryout," exclaimed her Aunt Dale. Ryane refused to make eye contact or acknowledge Justin's presence.

"Thank you, Aunt Dale," she said and went to their outdoor buffet table to get some potato wedges and bread where they were being kept warm.

"Justin, let me see if you have enough for my niece to have a snack later." He told her he did with his gaze fixed on Ryane. Her aunt stood in front of her to block his view while she checked his container and then put it in the shopping bag she had. "Yep, you do. I also have enough dessert for the both of you." He still stood waiting for Aunt Dale to move.

"Ryane, what is that on your finger, an engagement ring? Great day in the morning, that thing will blind you. Harry, get me my shades." She chuckled. Aunt Dale took her hand to examine it closely. I bet he wished he had left, thought her family, instead of standing there looking out of place. "Where is that fine thang?"

"Mama," said Lynn.

That was his cue to leave, thanking her aunt for the food.

"Well, he is. You welcome, Justin. Are you getting ready to go?" Aunt Dale said all that in one breath. Her aunt was a mess and everybody knew it.

"Yes, Aunt Dale, I'm going to check on my babies. I'll see you good people later."

"Okay, son. Enjoy."

He gave a nod and left.

"Now where was I? Oh, I know. I was asking about that fine man of yours," she said loud enough for him to hear.

182

"He's asleep, Aunt Dale, but I'll be sure to take him some food."

"Baby, I know you're some kind of special to that man, dropping down out of a helicopter like he did. I ain't gon' never forget that sight."

"Honey, you want me to drop out of a helicopter to show you how much I love you?"

"So you can break your fool neck and I have to take care of you for the rest of your life? No sir. Eat cha chicken."

Uncle Harry let out a hearty laugh with everyone joining in, and then went back to eating his chicken.

*

"Thank you, Ray Jr," said Ryane. "You don't know how much this means to us," she added and gave him a hug. Ryane, Chancey, and her parents watched as he got in his golf cart to drive off. He had taken over for his dad as the justice of the peace.

"Well, Babygirl, we're going to say good morning and get back in bed. Chancey, welcome to the family, son," said her daddy, giving him a pat on the back. "Need I say you've got my precious jewel and I'm depending on you to treat her right?"

"You can count on it, sir, and that's a promise," he said, shaking his hand. Ryan and Beverly Newton gave their daughter another hug and walked to their RV.

Ryane and Chancey had decided to exchange their

vows outside, behind their RV. They had complete privacy. It was a glorious, peaceful summer morning with God's magnificent nature as the perfect backdrop for their private ceremony. A slight breeze made it relatively comfortable as the moon shone brightly with the company of twinkling stars to provide natural light. You couldn't ask for more. All were asleep except the harmless serenading night creatures. Janice, Ray's wife, sent her a small bouquet of fresh flowers from her garden, which was sweet and thoughtful. Her parents waved as they stepped inside.

"Mrs. McGowan, are you ready for bed?" he asked, pulling off his shirt and throwing it on the sofa.

She looked at her handsome, sexy husband and whispered, "Yes." Besides, they were already dressed for bed. He had on his black, cotton silk pajama pants and she had on a short black satin, lace chemise, naturally with undergarments since her father and Ray were present. It was pure luck she packed it and she was certainly glad she did. When she told her mother they wanted them to be their witnesses and for them to keep on their pajamas, she was speechless. It was three o'clock in the morning and there wasn't a need to put clothes on. No one else would be present. Her father was happy he didn't have to dress and so was Ray.

CHAPTER TWENTY-ONE

Ryane put her flowers in a large drinking glass. Her husband took her hand and led her to their bedroom. She could hear the music being played as they entered. He turned the lights off, pushed a button to pull back the shade over the skylight, and caught her around the waist. Chancey pulled her to his chest; they began to slow dance to the love song that played. He hummed the melody against her ear. His rich, deep baritone voice infiltrated every nerve in her body. She kissed his naked skin and nipped the side of his neck as they swayed to the music.

He groaned, "Ooh girl, that feels good."

She stoked his powerful back down the center up to his shoulders while he continued to hum. He wanted to feel her soft, bare skin against his and pulled her chemise over her head, throwing it to the side. Her strapless bra was next. That's better, he thought but said aloud as they continued to dance, "Baby, if I knew the words to this song I would sing them to you."

She knew the words oh too well. This was Nanny and Pawpaw's CD and their song. She began to sing it to him. Her sweet, soulful voice was captivating as he held her tightly, pressing her breasts against him.

"...All I wanna do is sing about you... the sunshine you give mine... loving you is easier than breathing... I'll never sing another song about leaving... if someone would have told me that I would be behaving like I am... and here

I am with you… with you…

"Oh Ryane… girl I love you so much," he said, covering her mouth, kissing them both breathless with her holding on for support. Dancing, kissing, and caressing had them hot, steaming, and mindless…both craving for more. He turned her around, filling one hand with her fluffy, velvet breasts, plucking a nipple while stroking her jewels with the other. She moaned in delight, leaning back against him, moving seductively against his hardness. Rocky was ready and very much at attention.

"Mrs. McGowan, let's see if these Newton jewels have a new flavor," he said, suckling the side of her neck.

She gasped. "There's only one way for you to find out, Mr. McGowan." Once again taking her by surprise, he lifted her off her feet, walked to the bed, and sat her on the edge. This was something she was certainly going to have to get used to, she thought as she began to scoot back upon the bed.

He caught her leg. "Where are you going, Mrs. McGowan?"

She didn't have an answer.

He pulled her back until her legs were dangling down just like he wanted them. What he had planned for her would make her sit completely up. He eased her lace panties down, kissing what they had concealed. Her body arched as she felt his hot breath and lips. He then caressed and kissed each thigh and leg. He tested the jewels and knew she was ready, but not before he spoke what was in his heart. He stopped abruptly and walked over to his drawer.

"What are you doing?" she hissed breathlessly as she sat straight up. That was not what she had in mind.

"I need you to be patient, my sweets. I have something I want to say, but first I had to get this," he answered, holding up a little black pouch.

She was undecided as to whether she should pout or wait for another gift. Ohh…he can pick the most inappropriate times, she thought as her jewels continued to quiver. He sat beside her and leaned over to kiss her pouting lips. With a smile, he began to pleasure her with his touch while the words he spoke from his heart warmed her entire being…heart and soul. This *God* sent man had changed her whole life in four short months. Ryane thanked God silently as tears fell. She swallowed a cry while he added another exquisitely designed charm to her bracelet. He then took possession of her mouth in a lingering kiss, playing tag with her tongue. Trailing moist kisses from her neck to her jewels, leaving no skin untouched; turning her every way but loose, he began their lovemaking.

*

Ryane woke up alone and had to get her wits about herself. They'd spent the remainder of the morning participating in grown folks' fun with her passing smooth out. She didn't know how long she'd been sleep or when her husband left their bed, or what time of day it was. What she did know was her throat was dry and her legs were sore along with the *McGowan jewels,* as they were now called. And he said he and Rocky may not be up to par. Up to par, they were terrific. She just hoped her petroleum jelly was in her cosmetic bag, because right now she couldn't recall if she packed it or not. Smiling and looking at the fabulous wedding ring she was wearing, all Ryane Newton McGowan remembered was the awesome loving she was given. Mmmm, she could smell the aroma of barbecue and thought it was time to start her day. When she got up, she saw a shopping bag hanging on the rack and peeped inside to find her family t-shirt with a crinkled skirt.

Chancey heard the shower and knew she was finally up. His baby was exhausted and had every right to be. They'd made love until the sun hung high in the sky. Mrs. McGowan had a profound, passionate appetite, giving him one whooping good workout, he thought with a grin. He took a big swallow of water and went to check on her. She was nude, sitting on a towel trying to put body oil on her back. Pure temptation.

"Good afternoon, sleepy head."

She gasped. "Is it that late?" He was fully dressed and looked sexy as always, even in casual clothes. She was sure he was dressed like all the other men, denim, cropped cargo pants that stopped below his knees and a sleeveless family t-shirt.

"Just about," he said, taking her body oil. "Lay on your stomach, baby." He began massaging the light fragrance gently over her. His magical touch had her purring like a kitten. He turned her over to caress her perfumed soft skin with gentle kisses, lingering in certain places. She shuddered when his warm breath touched her skin. As if he gave her instructions, her legs spread. "You can just forget about that, Mrs. McGowan; your family is up and moving about." He kissed her lips and asked if she had anything for her tender area. She told him she had already taken care of that with a smile. "Good, now come on so I can help you get dressed. I'm ready to eat. Oh, did you see your shopping bag?" he asked, reaching for it. *So he's been shopping this morning.* He took out the t-shirt and skirt. "Your cousin Lynn had me buy you this skirt. She said it would probably be better suited and comfortable for you today."

Ryane gave him a suspicious look.

"What? I didn't say a word. And now I'm going to help you get dressed."

"Thanks, but that won't be necessary. Besides, you've already helped and did an excellent job; I can manage the rest alone."

"You mind if I watch, then?"

"Be my guest," she said with a cunning grin. "On second thought—" he jumped up before she could tell him what she wanted him to do. "Get my black underwear out of the drawer." She watched him move her things around and take out the lace cotton set. Ryane reached for her bra.

"I got it, baby."

If they planned to join the family, she was going to have to allow him to help. He put her bra in place like he'd had lots of practice, snapped it, and gently lifted her breasts to put them in the cup. Naturally, he couldn't pass

189

up kissing them and her. Her eyes fluttered shut. She swallowed hard as she always did whenever she felt his lips and hot breath on her bare skin. Next, he took her briefs and held them down for her to step in. He slowly pulled them up her legs and thighs until he had them in place, kissing every spot his hands touched. She moaned her husband's name several times as it became difficult for her to stand. She had to brace herself with her hands on his shoulders. He then took her skirt. "Really, I can take over from here," she panted.

"Oh, you don't want my help anymore?" he said, grinning.

"That's not it. You've turned a three-minute task into ten, and you did say you were hungry."

He burst into laughter as she swatted him on the shoulder. She shook her hand because of the pain. Ryane finally realized what he had been doing. "You've been teasing me the whole time." She snatched her skirt and shooed him away so she could put the rest of her clothes on. Once again, Lynn has done a fantastic job, thought Ryane as she slipped her feet into her red thong sandals. Their girly t-shirts were one of a kind. She fluffed the top of her half-dried curly hair, with a little oil, and added a color to her lips before leaving their bedroom.

*

Ryane and Chancey held hands as they walked to where her family had gathered under the pavilion for the festivities. Balloons and streamers were blowing from the commercial fans that cooled the hot summer day. Banquet tables were decorated with red and black ornaments.

190

Pans of barbecue, potato salad, baked beans, and desserts filled the buffet tables. Coolers with ice cold drinks were conveniently placed. The agenda was two-fold; families with children took their pictures first before they were allowed to enjoy carnival rides and eat. While that was going on, the others ate until it was their turn.

"Ryane... Ryane!" Once again, her name rang throughout the crowd with everyone looking in their direction. Her husband gave her an extra squeeze as she held on to him. Surveying the crowd, waving hands got her attention. It was Justin's family sitting at her parents table. Rena and Justin were missing. Before approaching the table, she recalled every precious word her husband said to her before they made passionate love... *I know this may not come off just right,"* he said clumsily. *"I hate what happened to you, because I witnessed first-hand the hurt and pain you endured because of it. But Ryane, to have you here with me as my wife, a part of my life, and having my baby, I'm forever grateful to Rena and Justin. I know that's totally selfish, but I would be lying if I wasn't honest about how I actually feel. I can only pray my love for you is strong and powerful enough for you to bury the past. And when you see them a few hours from now, instead of animosity and bitterness, silently thank God and offer them an olive branch of peace, absolute forgiveness, and love. It's because of them that we are one. Girl, I love you more than life itself. You hold my heart, my life, and all my love in the palm of your hands. And I'm willing to go through whatever, to have your love and ensure your happiness."* Then he gave her another charm for her bracelet, opened hands with a ruby shaped heart in the center. Her husband then went on to prove it by loving her with all his heart and soul...

"Ryane, we heard the good news," exclaimed Justin's sister, Linda. She was holding their new baby boy.

"Oh, Linda, he's beautiful."

"Just like his mother," said her husband Avery, giving Ryane a big hug and kiss. She introduced her husband while more hugs and well wishes were expressed, with her getting extra squeezes from the women in the family.

"Aunt Ryane, we miss you," exclaimed his nieces. She told the little people she missed them, too, giving each one a hug and kiss.

Somebody yelled for the entire Newton family to come have their pictures taken. The children cheered. They knew it would soon be time to open the carnival. Ryane assured them she would be back and took her husband's hand to follow the family. A repeat of embracing and well wishes was given to the newlyweds since she was the only one some of the family hadn't seen. The cousins wanted to see her gorgeous wedding ring and bracelet. Her solitaire was now surrounded by diamonds with the ring guard band. Everyone admired and made a big fuss over the size of her diamonds. Lynn and Darlene summed it up by saying she was the bling queen of the family. Rena and Justin stood aside watching, not knowing what to do although they sensed her demeanor was totally different. There was a peaceful calmness about her, almost like the old Ryane was present. But Justin didn't want to take any chances and kept his wife close to his side.

Pawpaw Newton wore the biggest grin ever, because he had all of his offspring there for the first time, with every grandchild and great-grandchild accounted for. Pictures were taken in order: Pawpaw and Nanny, their three sons, two daughters, and spouses, fifteen grandchildren and spouses, and thirty great-grands. It was a beautiful and precious sight; Nanny had to wipe his tears.

After the whole group was done, individual pictures were taken of the siblings and their families. Her father and his baby sister were last since they were not grandparents yet. Ryane sensed the tension and uncertainty on the faces of her grandparents. She knew they didn't know what to expect and were probably praying the *Holy Spirit* has consume her wholeheartedly.

Her father's name was finally called for their family portrait. Ryane took a deep breath and squeezed her husband's hand. She then walked over to take her place which was behind her daddy and next to her sister. She looked at her sister, patted her hand, and smiled. Her expression of compassion was too great for Rena. She was overwhelmed with emotions and began to sob.

Justin leaped to his feet to go to her, but Nanny stopped him as he watched his wife ease down on her knees with her arms around her sister's waist. He tried to protest, but Nanny held her ground as her eyes filled with tears. Ryane sat down and held Rena in her arms. Justin wiped a tear as he watched the woman he betrayed and hurt console his wife. His mother and father were now by his side.

"It's okay, Rena," Ryane whispered softly over and over while soothing her with tender strokes and caresses. Intense, heartfelt sobs shook Rena's body as she rocked and held on tightly to her big sister. You could hear their grandmothers praising *God* while witnessing what was transpiring—unconditional love and forgiveness—as the sisters continued holding on to each other. Beverly Newton was now in the arms of her new son-in-law, thanking him. Whether Chancey McGowan was aware of it or not, because of the love he had for their daughter, her family was now healed and whole, once again.

After the family's emotions were intact, the remaining pictures were taken of Ryan, Beverly, and their daughters. The sisters glowed with natural beauty as they stood with their parents and then their handsome husbands. Before leaving, the newlyweds took several separate pictures while receiving cat whistles and howls. Ryane and Chancey, in coordinating outfits, made a sexy and adoring couple during their poses. Ryane had no idea she had a performer on her hands. She had to remind him that her parents and grandparents were watching. But they were the ones urging him on. As always, their Nanny ended the picture taking session by calling for her grown and sexy girls, as she affectionately referred to her granddaughters. The women did their sexiest poses with Nanny leading the group. Pawpaw and the men whistled and howled as always, and the fun began.

CHAPTER TWENTY-TWO

The celebration weekend had come to an end for the McGowans and those family members who had fathers to visit today. Ryane and Chancey were on their way home so they could spend the remainder of Father's Day with his family. But not without making this a Father's Day her daddy would always remember. Ryan Newton was blown away and so was she when her husband gave their RV to him as a gift. He actually had tears.

The Newton and Alexander families along with their guests agreed this was the best Juneteenth and Father's Day celebration ever. Her grandfathers received their normal gifts of cash and gift cards. The holiday had been perfect for her, also. She was going back to Allanville with a peaceful mind and a totally different spirit. Most of all, she had a wonderful, kind, and generous husband whom she adored, as well as her family...

Shelly and Jackie almost had strokes when she gave them the news. They spoke on three-way so Ryane wouldn't have to repeat herself while she and her husband waited to board their flight. She promised to get back with Jackie tomorrow and would see Shelly at work some time Monday.

The day continued to bring about more surprises. The Judge made an announcement that he had decided to downsize and move into an apartment at Manor Hill's senior citizen residence. Both of his namesakes displayed cheesy grins and agreed silently that the old man had decided to start dating. They knew he had an ulterior motive when he invested in the building project with the Mitchells. He was also making the McGowan estate a gift to the newlyweds. He said the large stately house had been built with the mindset of raising lots of children, and he was depending on them to do just that. The ecstatic couple promised to put forth every effort before leaving for home.

*

"All right, you're going to lift me off the floor one time too many and won't be able to keep your promise to the Judge."

"I had to carry my bride across the threshold."

Mmmm, that's right, she was his bride. Although she didn't have any pictures of them exchanging their vows, the bling she was wearing was a constant reminder.

"I still say you better be careful," she said and closed the door behind them.

"You didn't know you married Superman's half-brother and side kick?" he said with a slick grin, pressing her against the door. He began kissing her fervently. She didn't have to ask who his side kick was as she put her arms around his neck while she welcomed his touch and kisses. Unbuttoning his shirt and easing it off while suckling a taunt nipple was causing him to become anxious. He walked her over to the sofa and pulled the tie to her peach wrap dress. Letting it fall to the floor, she began to strip him of his clothes while he relieved her of her matching undies. Discarded clothing was now in a pile out of their way. He held a breast in each hand as he

196

licked and sucked her tattooed skin. Straddling his lap she felt just what her jewels were yearning for, Rocky's hardness. She loved feeling him swell, and he knew it, doing a hard thrust and then a slow grind with her keeping up with his tempo. He released her breasts and took her hands to pin them behind her with his powerful arms. She liked that, too, and so did he, tightening his hold while doing his triple whammy, pumping, thrusting, grinding; causing them both to fill the room with booming cries as thunderous, raw passion consumed them.

*

Four weeks later

Ryane and Chancey were now settled and living in the McGowan mansion. They'd already had their first social event as husband and wife, the Fourth of July bash with his family and neighboring friends, and were looking forward to many other holidays and functions.

The newlyweds were happy to show off their new home. The beautiful country manor had already gone through major renovations a few years earlier. The attic had been turned into Chancey's domain with an outside entrance. They moved his complete, dark cherry wood sleigh bed set into the master suite. The expensive cherry wood furniture and floors throughout the house were perfect. Those pieces with an old rustic, stressed appearance, gave the place its old world charm. Naturally, the aged sofa and chairs needed a new look and were sent out to be reupholstered in colorful, family-friendly prints and solids. Heavy drapes were taken down and replaced with sheer window treatments and customized blinds. Chancey said he always regretted not remodeling the place sooner, at least before his grandmother passed. But both grandparents were creatures of habit and didn't like changes.

The Judge, himself, expressed how wonderful and refreshing the placed now looked. They told him his bedroom was still in the same place. But like all the other nine bedrooms, his bed coverings had been replaced with a bright and cheerful new bed set. All the rooms were done in lively, vivid colors that were charming and inviting. The screened-in back porch was the talk, being the most popular spot with its ceiling fans and light gray comfortable seating. To give the area a relaxing country retreat feeling, old number two tubs were used as flower pots with lush greenery and colorful blooms.

*

"Will you please take that grin off your face?" hissed Shelly as they sat on the bench in front of the hotel. Ryane couldn't help it if her husband made her smile. He called to say he was on his way to pick them up. They were leaving for Texarkana to spend the weekend. She promised Rena she would be there for her baby shower, and was able to twist Shelly's arm to go, since Jackie and her cousins were anxious to meet her new bud.

It was a clear evening, just right for flying, according to her husband. Yep, her husband also had his own plane. This was going to be their first time out in it. Ryane was blown away, along with his grandfather and parents, when he disclosed his assets and how much he was actually worth. He'd done well with his trust funds, investing them wisely.

"There he is," said Shelly, standing. She didn't know who had the biggest smile as she watched him stop his vehicle to get out. Ryane and Chancey exchanged a tender kiss and caress. *Talk about being in love; they were the poster couple.* She was happy for her girl, because she had been through a terrible storm. Shelly Roberts could only wish she was next. *Humph, in a pig's eye.* She'd already put a period behind the last guy she dated. It was now up to Edward Albert to pique her interest and keep it. So far, he was doing a pretty good job.

"Hey, Shelly, let me have your bag." He clearly snapped her out of her hopeless thoughts.

"Hi, Chancey, and thanks," she said, giving him her traveling bag. Shelly really didn't feel up to doing anything this weekend, but was glad Ryane and Jackie insisted she come, especially since she didn't have to pay for anything. The McGowans—own a plane—now that's truly something, she thought, getting into his SUV…

Pulling into the garage of the private airstrip in Hempstead, Chancey pointed out the plane as he got out and opened his wife's door. It was beautiful; neither Ryane nor Shelly was a bit surprised of its name, Chocolate Swirl. A fine brother with a cool swag who was dressed like Chancey, in jeans, a cream polo, and chocolate cap approached the SUV; no doubt he was his co-pilot. He opened Shelly's door and extended his hand…

"Okay, ladies, now that you've had the grand tour, have a seat and buckle up so we can be on our way," said

199

Chancey. But before going to the pilot's cabin, he made sure they were secured. Minutes later, they heard the engine and Chancey announced their arrival time and informed them that when the green light flashed, they could get up for refreshments or to use the facilities. He was a joke, thought Ryane and Shelly as they waited to unfasten their seatbelts to have a snack. It was no denying what was obvious; Mr. McGowan had something to be proud of. The *Chocolate Swirl* was not just a plain little airplane; it was a posh baby jet. Besides the pilot and co-pilot, the plane could seat eight people comfortably. Naturally, it had a lavatory and galley with other amenities for added comfort.

CHAPTER TWENTY-THREE

"Look at you," shouted the women in her and Justin's families. All were present except Rena. Ryane went around giving each one a hug with them all taking turns to rub her protruding stomach. Ryane introduced Shelly with everyone expressing how happy they were to finally meet her new best friend. It was evident why Ryane was portraying a bolder new look, the influence of her new best friend. Both ladies had on blue capris and designer tops with one bare shoulder in different colors and styles. Shelly's was short in the front with an extended back and Ryane's was a full tunic with a pointed hem. Both wore large hoop earrings and blue jeweled slides. When Jackie got a chance, she told Ryane she was right about Shelly having a combination of their personalities. Jackie had always tried to get her to put a little pizazz in her dress.

"Where's Rena?" asked Ryane.

Her mother said she was getting dressed again.

The room was smartly decorated in yellow and blue flowers, balloons, uniquely created mobiles of little t-shirts, bibs, and socks of various sizes...The Conners were having a boy. While they waited for the mother-to-be, they all wanted to know how Ryane was enjoying married life. She told them she loved every minute of it.

"I know you are, being married to that fine thang," exclaimed her Aunt Dale.

"All right, Mama, don't start," scolded Lynn. But everyone knew Aunt Dale was a mess. She was a chip off the old block, her mother... their Nanny.

"Anyway, where is he?" Darlene asked.

"Oh, you didn't know," said Lynn. "He picked up our grandfathers and the other men who were here and took them for a ride in *Chocolate Swirl*... their private airplane."

"Get outta here," screamed the women. Her cousins looked at her in total surprise, because not one time had she uttered a word during any of their telephone visits. Stella wanted to know what kind of house they lived in, and said a mansion, not knowing she was right on the money...

Shelly didn't hesitate to tell her she was correct, because she knew Ryane was not going to call it what it really was, a mansion. She also told them it was a beautiful landmark built in the early fifties that had been restored. It was absolutely gorgeous with a winding staircase and a tucked away elevator. They all gasped and whispered *OMG*, with one of them saying Ryane was living large. Her mother and grandmothers had wide grins on their faces for their own personal reasons. Rena finally made her appearance, looking like a doll in her yellow and blue, polka dot smock dress. She walked right up to her sister; they embraced and felt each other's stomach.

"Okay, the guest of honor has finally graced us with her appearance; let's get this party going."

"Wait, Nanny, I want to show Ryane the nursery that she paid for." She took her sister's hand to lead her to the room with Nanny telling them they had five minutes.

Ryane signaled for Shelly to come also. "Oh Rena, it's beautiful. I'm glad you decided to buy the light oak instead of something dark."

The room was completely furnished with baby furniture and a big rocker. The ladies walked around, touching, feeling, admiring, and voicing their favorite items. Ryane stroked the blue, print comforter and fluffed the little pillow.

"Now, this is too cute," said Shelly, fingering the soft musical mobile made out of fabric.

"Okay Rena, it's time for you to get off your feet," ordered Nanny, standing in the doorway. "You all can visit the nursery later."

When they walked in, everyone began to clap. "Here, sit on the loveseat Rena, and Ryane, you sit beside her," instructed their mother. Their mother then pinned a corsage made of hundred dollar bills and ribbon on Rena's chest. She and the guests gasped.

"Ryane, it's beautiful, thank you." She leaned over and kissed her sister. Her corsage which resembled a carnation was a work of art, thanks to Bubba Jenkins. The man was definitely talented.

"You're welcome, *little big sister.*"

"Oh Ryane," cried Rena as she hugged her sister. Some of her family members wiped away tears. Never did the family or friends think they would ever hear those words spoken for some years, at least. But Ryane Newton McGowan was no longer holding the past against her sister and brother-in-law. Because of them, she was living a blessed life with a wonderful man and expecting twins. She gave her sister an extra squeeze and the shower began.

CHAPTER TWENTY-FOUR

"Auh, Chancey, how long are you going to be gone this time?" whined Ryane as she stroked her husband's chest. "We have two appointments this week. The ultrasound is scheduled for Thursday, and the photographer will be here Friday." Ryane hated these impromptu assignments and was glad working with the special task unit would soon be over. She wanted her husband to be happy but hated when risk or danger was involved. But as he pointed out, people take risks every day. You never know when danger is lurking around the corner. She had to admit he was so right. Trisha Jenkins had no idea danger was waiting on her when she went to meet her brother at the property they had purchased.

He kissed her nose. "Baby, this is the last assignment and it's just for two days at the most. I'll be back; that's a promise." Capt. McGowan finally had a reason to make a career change and had put in his resignation with the task force which would take effect after this job, but he would remain in the reserves. He had a family to consider and was not taking any unnecessary chances being away from her and the babies. The Waller County sheriff's department had asked him to consider being a contractual helicopter pilot. He didn't have to give it much thought since flying was one of his passions. The job would also give him flexibility which would allow venturing out in a couple of business projects he was considering. "Don't make this any harder for me than it already is," he said, kissing her pregnant belly. "Come on, walk me to the door."

*

"Ryane, if he said he'll be here, you know he's coming," said Shelly, opening the door.

All she could do was nod her head like a child, because she was near tears as they pulled up to the clinic. Even though he'd never missed an appointment, there was always a first time. This was a special visit. Dr. Holly was sure she'd heard an extra heartbeat at their last visit and scheduled another ultra sound. In the beginning, they knew there were two babies. But now she wasn't so sure with the size of her very pregnant belly, but they would know definitely today. Hopefully, they would also know whether they had one of each or two of the same; that was if the little darlings were positioned right. She just hated to go in without him. But like her BF said, he had not disappointed her thus far, even with the special assignments he'd been involved in.

"Is that a helicopter I hear?" asked Shelly. Yes, it was, thought Ryane as she stepped back. Several other people walked out of the building to see. Across the street on a vacant lot, a helicopter hovered low. A ladder dropped and then that fine husband of hers climbed down, dressed in his combat gear. She watched him run across the street with a big smile. He was here.

"Hey, Baby," he said, giving her a squeezing hug and kiss. "I told you I would be here."

Ryane felt so fortunate to have this wonderful and caring man in her life and was finally able to actually say how grateful she was to Rena and Justin for the part they played. Like her husband said on their wedding night, if it hadn't been for them, their paths never would have crossed.

"Come on, let's go have that ultrasound so I'll know for sure how many mouths I'm going to feed." They laughed and went inside…

"Doc, is that three little heads?" asked Chancey as he got closer to the screen.

"I'm afraid not, Chancey. You see four! You're going to have quadruplets!"

"Four babies, four babies," he repeated himself and held up four fingers as if that was the only way for the news to register. "Thank you, baby," he said, kissing his wife who wore a big smile on her face. "Girl, if this is the way you're going to do it, we'll only have to go through this one more time and we'll be done with our big family. And most of all, the old man will be one happy dude with all the little people running around."

Ryane's smile disappeared immediately with Chancey and Dr. Holly bursting into hearty laughter.

*

For the last three months, Ryane had everyone's sympathy due to her heavy load, and was treated like a porcelain doll. Nevertheless, other than the extra weight, she had a smooth pregnancy with minor complications regardless of her carrying four. Naturally, the McGowan men insisted she cut down her work load to four hours, three days a week once it was confirmed she was carrying quadruplets. And at the end of October, they suggested strongly she take an early maternity leave.

Everything was now ready for the McGowan children, including a customized luxury van. Thanks to *Baby World* and the hard work of Godmother Shelly and the babies' grandmothers, a beautifully furnished nursery was complete. It was done in lively pastel shades of rose, blue, and yellow since the sexes of two of the babies were still unknown. The room across from the master suite was designated for the babies for now, with future plans for expansion once they had outgrown their baby beds. As for names, they had four for each sex. The *Chanceys* didn't want to continue with number five since they knew two of the babies were boys. It would be perfect if the other two were girls, but Nanny cautioned her not to get her hopes up. She would certainly have to go down this road once more for her little girl, but no way soon. Four babies were going to be a handful, even if they did have a live-in nanny and two part-time assistants.

*

"Sweetie, is there anything I can do for you?" asked her husband.

"Yes, tell Dr. Holly to deliver these babies tomorrow."

He kissed her gently and caressed her huge middle. "We'll see," he said, nuzzling her cheek.

Ryane and Chancey were anticipating Dr. Holly's visit that night to give them her decision as to when she was going to do the C-section. Ryane had been admitted to the hospital four days ago. Both families were anxiously waiting and ready for the babies to make their grand appearance. Her parents, Rena, Justin and Baby JR had arrived today thanks to her wonderful husband. That was her early *Christmas* present. He was trying desperately to make their first *holiday* as festive as possible, since they would be spending it in Cypress Memorial. Jenkins Florist had delivered a beautiful tree for her room to help keep her in the holiday spirit. There were also cards galore expressing congratulations and wishing them happy holidays.

After a soft knock, the door opened. Her doctor stuck her head in. She didn't know what to expect with Mr. McGowan around. "Hey, you two, that's how you got here in the first place," chuckled Dr. Holly. "Okay, Ryane, we're going to relieve you of your load first thing in the morning," stated the doctor. "Is eight o'clock too early?"

Tears of happiness filled her eyes; she wiped them as they fell. Chancey flashed a huge grin before he pressed his lips against the tears she missed. They both thanked the doctor for the wonderful news, and she told them goodnight.

"Well, baby, this is it," Chancey said excitedly as he texted the good news. The precious McGowan babies would be delivered two days before Christmas, practically on schedule. The words spoken by her doctor were pure joy and a blessing for an overly anxious mother and an ecstatic daddy...

The lobby was filled with family and friends who were waiting impatiently for Dr. Holly to inform them that the babies were delivered, and Ryane was fine. Chancey and the men took turns standing close to the delivery room door, peeping in the window.

"I see her doctor," announced Chancey.

Dr. Holly waved with a huge smile displayed on her face. These were her first set of quad. She was proud and felt honored to have had the privilege of delivering them. Chancey stepped away from the door with the family now by his side.

"Well, Mr. McGowan, it's all over; your sons and their mother are just fine."

"Sons!" he shouted. "Sons, all four are boys! Four boys, you hear that, I got four sons," he exclaimed as he turned to face the family. "My wife, when can I see her?"

"She's in recovery right now. It will be a few minutes before she returns to her room and then you can see her. The nurses are getting the babies ready now."

He grabbed Dr. Holly and lifted her completely off the floor, twirling her around.

"Chancey McGowan, if you don't put me down!" He did and she patted him on the back. "I'll send the nurse out to let you know when you can see your boys."

He thanked her again and then went into his happy dance, chanting to his own special beat, "I'm the man...I got four hardheads...I'm the man." He danced, stomped, and bumped fists with the men and kissed the women all the way over to a chair to get a large gift bag. Inside it were chocolate swirl pops he had made especially for the occasion. Pink and blue ribbons engraved with the words *Baby McGowan* were wrapped around each candy stick. He began to pass them out as he swaggered around the room like the proud father he was.

"One for you, one for you—" he was interrupted by a nurse. He gave her one, too.

"Mr. McGowan, you and your family may see the babies, now. And your wife will be ready in about ten minutes, sir."

Chancey looked at his excited family members, who were thrilled, and told them to go ahead, he and Ryane would see them together. He watched his family rush around to the nursery with him going in the direction of Ryane's room to wait for her. A few minutes later, the nurse and orderly brought Ryane in.

"I need to warn you, Mr. McGowan, she's still a little drowsy."

He grinned. "That's au'right, she earned the right," he said and presented them a chocolate swirl pop too. He walked over to her bed, leaned over, and gently nudged her cheek and kissed her lips. "I love you, Mrs. McGowan. Thank you for my sons."

"You're welcome, Mr. McGowan. Have you seen them yet?" she asked, fluttering her eyes open, gazing into his handsome loving face. She looked around; more flowers along with balloons festively decorated had been added. And there was her BF who was taking her responsibility of picture-taking serious. She had been designated the job of capturing all the memories for the photo albums and she hadn't missed one single moment.

He held her hand and pressed his lips against hers. "No, I thought we'd see them together," he said and slipped an exquisite, large blue topaz surrounded by four diamonds on her finger. It was her mother's ring.

"Oh Chancey, it's beautiful; thank you, sweetie."

"I would ask how you feel, but I know the answer to that after having four hardheads."

"Don't call my babies that."

"That's what cha say now." He chuckled.

There was a knock, then the door swung open.

"We have four little darlings who want their mommy and daddy," sang the nurses.

The family stayed in the lobby to give the new parents a few minutes of privacy. One of the nurses adjusted Ryane's bed just a bit so she could hold them for a few minutes so that Shelly could take the first mommy pictures.

"Auh, Chancey, look, they are just beautiful."

He was lost for words as tears rolled down his face.

When he was finally composed, he whispered, "Baby, they really are and so are you." He gently embraced mother and sons while Shelly took pictures. Humph, *I'm the man Captain Chancey McGowan* had wimped totally out at the sight of his precious boys will be the caption for this shot, thought Shelly.

*

March 21, first day of spring

The McGowans had a house full with four RVs on the property. Her Texarkana family came down during their spring break week. The Newtons and Alexanders had been entertained well. To bring their visit to a close, Chancey and his dad were throwing a barbecue, Texas style, with all the trimmings.

"Where are my godsons?" Shelly asked as she entered the McGowan's home.

Ryane stared at her in disbelief. She was carrying a large gift bag. They were going to need a storage room for all the baby things if her family and their godmother don't stop with all the gifts.

"I know what you're going to say, but I just couldn't leave them in the store. Anyway, they have to grow into them." Shelly not only bought an outfit, she also got shoes, socks, and caps.

"Really, godmother," scolded Ryane.

Shelly turned, leaving her glaring at the back of her head. She joined the others in the large family room where portable cribs were set up. Of course they were empty with all the family around. Needless to say, the little darlings were already spoiled rotten and insisted on being in someone's arms unless they were put in something with a rocking motion.

"Hey, Shelly," greeted everyone.

She worked the room with hugs and kisses. "Oh, look at my babies; they look so cute." They had on striped yellow and blue onesies with socks to match. "Godmother

213

hasn't seen her boys in two whole days. I missed you so."
She went around and kissed the back of each one's bald
head. "I'm next," she said excitedly.

"Girl, you can have Chadwyck now. He needs a
serious diaper change," exclaimed Ryane's cousin, Stella.
Everyone was shocked when she even decided to make
the trip but then, too, they really weren't. Her sole purpose
was to see for herself how her cousin was living. Ryane
heard her and knew the other three would need a diaper
change also.

"That's all right, my godmother don't mind changing
my *diapee*...no she don't."

Ryane joined her, singing the same tune,
"Momma's boys need their diapee changed...yes they do."
She reached for Chandler and Chancelor, who began to
coo at the sound of her voice.

"I'll change my own baby," exclaimed Lynn and
Jackie.

"Nanny, let me have Charlton so you won't have to
get up."

"Just be sure you give him back to me. We're still
bonding."

"I will, Nanny."

The ladies went to the downstairs baby room to
clean the boys up. Ryane reminded Jackie and Lynn
about them. They had already caught them with their
guards down once. "You betta watch me, Auntie Jackie
and Auntie Lynn, I'ma squirter and I have perfect aim...
yes, I do...our momma said so...she said she's tired of

214

looking at little Rockies…yes, she did." The boys cooed, waved their little hands, and kicked their little feet as if they knew what she said.

The ladies giggled, not knowing Chancey was standing in the doorway. Any other time, his male scent would have given him away, but not with this diaper change. He walked up behind his wife and wrapped his arms around her waist. Startled, she quickly turned her head to the side and looked into the face of her handsome husband.

"Surely, you don't mean that, baby," he said while pulling her against his hard body, nibbling and kissing her ear.

Giving him a wink with a smile, she answered in her baby voice, "Momma said little, Daddy."

Dear Reader

Wasn't Chancey McGowan really something? Talking about a Black Knight driving a Porsche, yeah right only in romance novels and movies. Anyway I hope you enjoyed Ryane and Chancey's story. Naturally we will visit them and the quads as Shelly's story unfolds. And yep the Allanville's Matchmakers finally found the perfect man for Dana Mitchell. She really put them through the ringer.

I love hearing from readers, so drop me a few lines. I'm on face book now, Author W Parks Brigham.

Lots of love and romance to ya!

Email address wparksbrigham@writeme.com

W Parks Brigham

 PO Box 330353

Houston, Texas 77233

Other available books by W PARKS BRIGHAM

DESTINED TO BE….REIVISED (2011)

PROMISES (2012)

WHO AM I SUPPOSE TO LOVE? (2013)

SURVIVING THE STORM (2014)

YOU WERE MEANT FOR ME (2014 Allanville Matchmakers Series Book #1)

YOU BELONG TO ME (2014 Allanville Matchmakers Series Book #2)

Look for these releases in the near future.

YOU'RE THE ONE FOR ME (Allanville Matchmakers Series Book #4)

New release of *SENSELESS MISCONCEPTIONS*